Love,
Ellie

H. Moore

So great to meet you!
H. Moore

To Ronnie

CONTENTS

1 APARTMENT 4B
<u>2005</u>

Ellie Hart had never pictured herself here — forty-nine years old, balancing a box of books against her hip, starting over in a place that felt foreign and unfamiliar.

The building rose above her like something out of a forgotten novel — old brick softened by time, ivy climbing in graceful spirals, tall windows framed by wrought-iron balconies.
Historic, elegant — the kind of beauty that bore its scars proudly.

She pushed open the heavy iron gate with her shoulder. The courtyard was quiet, framed by worn brick and the hush of early evening. The leaves shivered in the breeze like they were whispering secrets she wasn't ready to hear.

She had been betrayed before.
Small betrayals at first — her first love, who cheated on her when she was out of town for her grandfather's funeral. The man she dated in her twenties who proposed to her, then stole money from her and ran off with a coworker. The colleague who promised to build a life together, then treated her body like a possession and her soul like an afterthought.

1

Each time, she lost a little more of herself.
Each time, it took a little longer to trust again.

Ellie had stopped believing in the kind of love people swore lasted forever.

Her poems, once full of soft hope and open-ended longing, grew sharper, sadder, harder-edged.

Ironically, it was some of her best work — fueled by the high-octane pain of disillusionment she could never quite outrun.

And then came Mark.

Mark was different.

He wasn't loud or flashy.
He was steady. Thoughtful.
The kind of man who noticed that she liked two sugars in her coffee, who bought her a copy of her favorite out-of-print poetry collection just because he "happened to find it," who told her — quietly, reverently — that he loved her and that he was going to put her on a better path in life.

Sure, there were red flags. He had been married twice before.

He wasn't the best communicator, and he didn't fawn over her or make grand declarations.

His love was quieter than that — steady, thoughtful, slipping into her life so naturally it was easy to believe it had always been there.

Still, it was a beautiful whirlwind — but not the reckless kind.
It was the kind that made her feel *safe* for the first time in her life.

At first, it terrified her.

Trust was not something Ellie gave easily anymore.
There were nights she lay awake beside him, feeling the thud of her own heart against the dark, waiting for the inevitable disappointment she was sure would come.

But Mark was patient.
He stayed.
He loved her through it.

Looking back now, there had been signs of what to come.

The way Mark spoke over her in conversations.

That one night she spent ages picking out a sexy outfit, only to be met with a shrug and a distracted glance.

The way he talked about other women — how "hot" they were — like she wasn't standing right there.

The way he scanned the room at parties, eyes always moving past her.

The slow fade of the kisses that used to make her dizzy.

And always, always, the promise of "later."
Later, they'd move in. Later, they'd talk about marriage. Later. Later. Later.

But Ellie had learned to explain away small heartbreaks.
She told herself all relationships settled eventually.
She told herself that comfort was a kind of love, too.

She stayed.
For twelve years, she stayed.

Until the night she found the message.

It happened on an ordinary night — the kind you never expect will be the one that ruins you.

Mark's phone buzzed on the kitchen counter while he was out walking the dog.
A name she didn't recognize.
A message she was never meant to see.

Can't stop thinking about last night. Miss you already.

The words weren't explicit.
That was the worst part.
They were tender — intimate in a way that made Ellie feel like an intruder in her own life.

When Mark came home, brushing snow off his jacket, smiling like nothing had changed, she felt something inside her quietly crack.

She set the phone on the table between them.

She didn't yell.
She didn't cry.

She just waited.

Mark's face crumpled — not with shame.
Not even with regret.
With inconvenience.
As if she had caught him at a bad time.

And in that moment, Ellie understood something that would burn inside her for months afterward:

It was never love.
Not really.
It was comfort.
It was convenience.
It was a place for him to rest until something easier came along.

Later, when she packed her boxes — books, notebooks, framed
photographs that suddenly meant nothing — she thought about how
small she'd become for him.
How careful.
How accommodating.
How she had made herself less so he could feel like more.

And she hated him for it.
But she hated herself more.

Not for loving him.

For trusting him with all the parts of herself he had never deserved to
hold.

Now, months later, she was here.

Starting over.
Alone.
At forty-nine.

No husband.
No children.
No tidy ending.

Just herself — and whatever pieces of her heart she could salvage.

2 THE KINDNESS OF STRANGERS

Ellie balanced the last of the moving boxes on her hip, nudging the heavy iron gate open with her shoulder. The courtyard smelled of damp stone and early spring — earthy, green, alive.

She paused for a moment, letting the gate clang shut behind her, breathing it all in.
It was the first time in a long while she had stood still without feeling the weight of somewhere else she was supposed to be. No deadlines. No packed schedules. Just this: a courtyard that smelled like rain and promise.

"Need a hand?"

The voice was warm, casual — the kind that made you look up even before you realized someone was talking to you.

Ellie turned. A man was crossing the courtyard toward her, hands tucked in the pockets of a worn gray hoodie, jeans slightly frayed at the cuffs. There was an easy confidence to his stride, but none of the arrogance she had grown used to sidestepping.

She shifted the box to get a better grip. "I'm good, thanks."

He grinned. "You *say* that now, but wait until you hit the stairs."

Ellie laughed despite herself — a soft, surprised sound. "Fair point."

He reached out instinctively, steadying the top box as it wobbled. His fingers brushed hers — just for a second — and Ellie stiffened, every nerve ending still frayed from the life she'd just walked away from.

She drew in a breath she hadn't realized she was holding.

"Thanks," she said quickly, almost too quietly.

He just smiled — easy, patient — and stepped back, giving her space.

It was the first kindness she had encountered in what felt like a very long time.

"I'm Jamie," he said.

"Ellie."

They stood there for a moment, each balancing a polite smile, the way strangers do when the conversation could either end or stumble forward.

"You just move in?" Jamie asked, nodding toward the building.

"Today," Ellie said. She looked up at the weathered brick, the faded paint around the windows, the ivy that climbed stubbornly no matter how many times it was trimmed back. "Feels like the kind of place that's seen a lot of lives pass through."

Jamie followed her gaze. "Yeah. Some places hold onto stories."

He said it casually, but something about the way he said it made her chest ache a little — a feeling she couldn't name, like nostalgia for a memory she hadn't made yet.

"Well," he said, stepping back, "welcome to the madhouse."

Ellie smiled. "Thanks. I'll try to fit in."

He gave her a mock-serious look. "If you hear someone playing bad guitar through the walls... that's probably me. Sorry in advance."

Ellie laughed again, lighter this time, the box shifting in her arms. Jamie caught it easily, steadying her once more without making a big deal of it.

"You sure you don't want a hand?"

She hesitated. Pride was a stubborn thing. But something about Jamie made her feel — not foolish for needing help, but... understood. Seen.

"Maybe just to the elevator," she said.

"Deal."

As they crossed the courtyard together, Ellie glanced sideways at him. There was nothing extraordinary about him at first glance — messy dark hair, sneakers scuffed at the toes, a face that would get better-looking the longer you knew it.
But there was something else.
A kindness in the way he moved.
A steadiness that was easy to miss if you weren't looking for it.

She didn't believe in fate. Not really.
But later — much later — Ellie would remember that afternoon and wonder if the ivy had whispered a secret she was too new, too guarded, to hear.

Look. Here he is.

3 IT'LL FEEL LIKE HOME

The elevator wheezed like an old man climbing stairs, jerking to a stop on the fourth floor. Ellie gripped the worn brass railing, balancing the box on her hip, while Jamie leaned casually against the opposite wall, arms crossed, watching her with a crooked smile.

"Fourth floor," he said. "Good choice. Less foot traffic. Better sunsets."

Ellie shifted the box to free one hand, pushing the stray hair from her forehead. "And here I thought I chose it because it was the only unit without a broken dishwasher."

Jamie grinned. "That too."

The doors rattled open, revealing a long hallway lined with mismatched rugs and doors painted in varying degrees of cream. Ellie stepped out first, feeling the strange vulnerability of not knowing exactly where her new life would fit in.

"Which one's yours?" Jamie asked.

"4B," she said, nodding toward the far end.

Jamie gave a low whistle. "Prime real estate. You're right across from Mrs. Donnelly."

Ellie raised an eyebrow.

"You'll hear her parakeet before you meet her. Looks like a tennis ball, screams like a banshee."

Ellie laughed, the sound echoing softly down the hall. She hadn't realized how much she'd missed laughing like this — the easy kind that didn't feel like an obligation.

She stopped in front of her door, setting the box down with a soft thud. Fishing for her keys, she glanced at him.
"You're not a salesman for the building, are you?"

Jamie smiled. "Full disclosure: I'm not even a very good neighbor. I'm the guy who forgets to pick up packages for days."

"Good to know," Ellie said, unlocking the door. She pushed it open with her foot, revealing a beautiful sunlit corner unit — wood floors, high ceilings, and a single wide window with sheer curtains billowing in the breeze.

Jamie peeked inside. "Nice bones."

Ellie shrugged. "It'll feel like home eventually."

He hesitated for a second, then said, "If you ever need help unpacking... or, you know, if your dishwasher explodes, I'm usually around."

Ellie turned to look at him — really look.
There was no pressure in his offer. No expectation. Just a kind of quiet willingness that felt rare in a world where everyone seemed to want something.

"Thanks," she said, meaning it.

For a moment, neither of them moved. The breeze tugged at the curtains, carrying with it the faint smell of the lavendar growing wild below.

"I should let you get settled," Jamie said finally, rocking back on his heels. "But welcome, Ellie."

He said her name like it meant something.

"Thanks, Jamie."

He flashed her a quick smile — the kind you didn't realize you'd memorized until later — and walked back down the hall, whistling a tune she couldn't quite place. Daydream Believer maybe?

Ellie stood in the doorway, her box forgotten at her feet, and watched him go.

4 THE SOUND OF SMALL THINGS

Ellie sat cross-legged on the hardwood floor, a battered cardboard
box open in front of her.
Books spilled out across the living room — novels, poetry
collections, old journals full of barely legible scribbles.
She ran her hand over the covers like they were old friends she
hadn't seen in years.

The late afternoon sun slanted through the wide window, casting
lazy, golden stripes across the floorboards.
Somewhere outside, a radio played — soft, a little crackly —
something old and low and comforting.
Maybe Johnny Cash. Maybe not.

She was just reaching for a slim volume of Emily Dickinson when
there was a knock at the door.

Ellie hesitated.
She rose slowly and pulled open the door.

Jamie stood there, holding a small potted plant — something leafy
and a little lopsided, as if it wasn't sure what direction to grow in yet.

"Welcome gift," he said, lifting it slightly. "I figured you're probably
knee-deep in boxes and could use something green."

Ellie blinked at him, momentarily at a loss.

"It's a pothos," Jamie added. "Practically indestructible. Good for people who have other things to worry about."

A smile tugged at the corner of her mouth before she could stop it.

"Thanks," she said, taking the pot carefully. The plant wobbled a little, as if it, too, was trying to find its footing.

Jamie rocked back on his heels. "Hope I'm not interrupting some great literary masterpiece in the making."

Ellie shook her head. "Just... trying to find space for old things."

He glanced past her into the apartment — the half-unpacked boxes, the piles of books.
His gaze wasn't judgmental.
It was... understanding.

"You settling in okay?" he asked.

Ellie shrugged. "Trying. Some days feel easier than others."

Jamie nodded like he knew exactly what she meant.

There was a pause — the kind that could have turned awkward if either of them had forced it.
But Jamie just stood there, easy and patient, letting the silence be what it was.

Finally, Ellie set the plant down carefully on the windowsill and said, "Do you want to come in for a minute? I can offer you bad coffee. Or slightly worse tea."

Jamie grinned. "Bad coffee sounds about right."

They sat on the floor, mugs balanced carefully on top of a closed box labeled *Kitchen Stuff*, the air between them loose and easy.

For a while, they talked about nothing important — the quirks of the building, the awful elevator, Mrs. Donnelly's screeching parakeet, the way the hallway always smelled faintly like vanilla candles and old books.

It was the first conversation Ellie had had in months that didn't feel like she had to perform.

She was halfway through a story about getting locked out of her old apartment when she caught herself laughing — *really* laughing — and felt the sting of tears at the edges of it.

She swallowed them down quickly, embarrassed.

Jamie must have noticed, but he didn't say anything.
He just took a sip of his terrible coffee and leaned back against the wall, giving her space to find her breath again.

In the fading light, Ellie realized something quietly astonishing:
She didn't feel like she had to be anything other than exactly who she was.

No explaining.
No justifying.
No shrinking.

Just... herself.

And for now, that was enough.

5 THE QUIET PLACES

The next few days passed in a soft blur.

Ellie spent her mornings unpacking and her afternoons wandering the neighborhood, mapping out the new rhythm of her life —the bookstore on the corner, the nearest grocery store, the coffee shop Jamie had recommended where the muffins really were better than the coffee.

The weather warmed slightly, enough that she could leave the windows open and let the scent of rain-soaked stone and blooming lavender drift in.

Sometimes, late in the afternoon, she could hear the faint sound of a guitar somewhere down the hall — not concert hall playing, not even trying for perfection — just the slow, easy strumming of someone who liked the way music filled up a room.

She found herself listening for it without meaning to.

It was early evening when she saw Jamie again.

She was sitting on the front steps of the building, a notebook open in her lap, pen tapping idly against the paper.
The pages were mostly empty — a few half-formed lines, a sketch of

an idea she hadn't been brave enough to finish yet.

Jamie came around the corner carrying a paper bag that looked suspiciously like takeout, a set of battered headphones around his neck.
He spotted her immediately and grinned.

"Didn't take you for a front steps kind of person," he said, stopping a few feet away.

Ellie smiled. "Trying to be less mysterious."

Jamie laughed and held up the bag. "Thai food. Highly suspicious, slightly addictive. Want some?"

Ellie hesitated.

In her old life, spontaneous invitations were rare. Everything had been planned, measured, transactional.
She wasn't sure she remembered how to just say yes without thinking it through a hundred different ways.

But something about Jamie — the easy way he stood there, no pressure, no expectation — made it feel less like a risk and more like a choice.

"Sure," she said, closing her notebook.

They sat side by side on the steps, passing containers back and forth — noodles, curry, crispy spring rolls that tasted better than anything that came from her own kitchen.

They ate mostly in silence, just two people sharing space, breathing the same evening air.

At one point, Jamie nudged her with his elbow. "You're a writer, right?"

Ellie glanced at him, startled. "What makes you say that?"

He shrugged. "Notebook. The faraway look. Plus, you have that 'please don't ask me what I'm working on' face."

Ellie laughed, genuinely amused. "Guilty."

"Anything good?"

She shook her head. "Mostly unfinished thoughts right now."

Jamie nodded like he understood.
"Those are the best ones," he said. "They haven't gotten scared yet."

Ellie stared at him, feeling something shift — a quiet place opening where fear used to live.

Later, as the sky turned violet and the streetlights flickered on, they packed up the empty containers and stood awkwardly for a moment at the bottom of the steps.

Jamie rubbed the back of his neck. "Thanks for sharing your staircase."

Ellie smiled. "Thanks for the suspicious noodles."

They lingered for a second longer than necessary —
not touching, not moving —something passing between them too soft to name yet.

Then Jamie tipped an invisible hat, grinning, and walked away.

Ellie watched him go, feeling lighter than she had in months.

The kind of lightness you didn't notice until you realized how long you'd been carrying weight.

She turned back toward the building, notebook forgotten under her arm, and let herself wonder — just a little — what might come next.

6 SKETCHES IN THE COURTYARD

The weather turned warm almost overnight, like the world had decided it was tired of pretending winter still had any say.

Ellie found herself spending more time outside — reading on the steps, scribbling in her notebook, simply sitting still in the courtyard as life moved around her.

She hadn't realized how much she missed being part of the small hum of ordinary things.

One afternoon, she rounded the corner of the building and stopped.

Jamie was there, sitting cross-legged on the flagstones, a battered sketchbook resting on his knees.
A set of charcoal pencils spilled out beside him, smudging the hem of his jeans.

He didn't see her at first.
He was too focused — head bent, hand moving quickly, almost fiercely, across the page.

Ellie hesitated, not wanting to disturb him.
But something about the scene held her in place — the easy way he moved, the way the late sun caught in the messy strands of his hair,

the complete lack of self-consciousness.

This wasn't someone showing off.
This was someone *being*.

After a moment, Jamie glanced up and caught her watching.

Instead of looking embarrassed, he smiled — wide, genuine, the kind that made his whole face lighter.

"Hey," he said, patting the ground beside him. "You're not interrupting."

Ellie crossed the courtyard slowly and sat down, smoothing her skirt underneath her.

Jamie flipped the sketchbook around and held it out.
It was a rough drawing of the courtyard — the crumbling stone benches, the stubborn ivy, the fountain that hadn't worked in years. But somehow, through the quick strokes and blurred lines, he had captured something Ellie hadn't been able to name — the feeling of the place.
The way it held you.
The way it made you believe, just a little, in second chances.

"You're good," Ellie said softly, handing it back.

Jamie shrugged like it wasn't anything.
"I just draw what's already there."

They sat for a while like that, side by side, letting the sun sink lower, the world go quieter.

Ellie found herself tracing the cracks in the flagstones with her fingertip, feeling a strange, steady warmth at the center of her chest.

Not the wild rush she had felt with other men —

Not the breathless, dangerous plunge she had been taught to mistake for love.

This was something quieter.

Something she could actually imagine surviving.

Jamie set his sketchbook aside and leaned back on his hands.

"You ever think about how places remember us?" he asked.

Ellie turned to him, surprised.

He wasn't smiling when he said it.
He was serious, thoughtful — like he was offering her something important.

"I think some places hold pieces of us," he went on. "The good parts. The ones we forget."

Ellie swallowed against the sudden ache in her throat.

Maybe that was why she had chosen this building.
Maybe that was why she hadn't been able to walk away the first time she stepped into the courtyard.

Maybe she needed a place to hold the parts of herself she was still too afraid to claim.

She looked at Jamie — really looked — and for the first time, she let herself wonder what it would feel like not to run.

Not to hold back.

Not to live always waiting for the other shoe to drop.

The air between them changed — just slightly.
Not enough for a stranger to notice.

But enough that Ellie felt it in the quickened beat of her heart.

She tucked her hair behind her ear, suddenly shy.

Jamie didn't move closer.
He didn't push.

He just waited — patient, steady — giving her all the space she needed to decide.

The courtyard smelled like rain and lilacs and new beginnings.

For the first time in a very long time, Ellie let herself believe in it.

Maybe not all at once.
Maybe not perfectly.

But enough.

Enough to stay.
Enough to hope.
Enough to begin.

7 A KISS UNDER THE STARS

Ellie hadn't planned on running into Jamie that evening, but she had hoped she would.

She had wandered into the courtyard after dinner, her hands wrapped around a chipped mug of tea, barefoot and pulled into an old cardigan that still smelled like cedar.

She didn't expect anyone else to be there.

But Jamie was.

He was sitting on the edge of the fountain — legs stretched long, elbows resting behind him — staring up at the night sky like it had something to say.

The broken fountain wasn't running, hadn't in years, but something about the way he sat there made it feel like it didn't matter. Like stillness had its own kind of magic.

He looked over when he heard her, a slow smile pulling at his mouth.

"I was hoping you'd come out."

Ellie paused in the archway, surprised. "You were?"

Jamie nodded, shifting to make space beside him. "You're kind of my favorite part of the building."

The words weren't smooth. They weren't even said with a wink.

They were just *true*, laid bare and uncomplicated in the quiet of the courtyard.

Ellie crossed the stones slowly, the mug warm in her hands.

"Careful," she said, settling beside him. "Flattery this early might give me the wrong impression."

Jamie glanced sideways at her, his voice low and almost playful. "What would the wrong impression be?"

"That you mean it."

He didn't laugh. Didn't deflect.

"I do."

Ellie blinked.

It was the kind of thing a different man might have said with an edge — a dare, a tug, a pressure. But Jamie didn't rush to fill the space after it. He let the words sit there like an open door.

Ellie took a slow breath and looked up at the stars. They were faint — city stars, dulled by light and life — but still stubbornly there.

"I don't know what I'm doing," she said finally. "I'm not sure I'm ready for… anything."

Jamie nodded. "I'm not asking for anything."

"But you want something."

He didn't deny it.

Instead, he tilted his head toward her, voice soft. "I want to know you."

Ellie looked down into her tea. "That's not a small thing."

"I know," he said. "That's why I'm not rushing it."

The air between them shifted again — warmer now, charged not with urgency, but with understanding.

Ellie set the mug beside her and pulled her knees up, wrapping her arms around them. "I've spent most of my life being someone else's version of safe."

Jamie was quiet for a beat.

Then: "I don't need you to be safe. Just honest."

She turned to him, surprised again by the way he said things — clear, quiet, never grasping.

"What if I don't know who I am when I'm honest?" she asked, only half joking.

Jamie's voice was steady. "Then we figure it out together."

There it was again — that *together*. That word she hadn't let herself believe in for so long.

A breeze stirred the ivy above them, and somewhere in the distance, a wind chime clinked like glass laughter.

Jamie reached into his hoodie pocket and pulled out a folded scrap of paper.

"I sketched this earlier. Wasn't sure if I should show you."

Ellie took it carefully. It was a quick sketch of her — sitting on the steps earlier that week, notebook in hand, hair caught in the wind.

It wasn't perfect.

But it was *real*.

He had drawn the way she looked when she didn't know anyone was watching.

She stared at it for a long moment, a lump rising in her throat.

"You see me," she said softly.

Jamie shrugged, but his eyes were serious. "I try to."

Ellie reached for his hand.

She didn't overthink it.

Didn't analyze what it meant or where it was going.

She just... held it.

And Jamie held back.

Not tightly.

Just enough.

They sat there as the night deepened around them, stars blinking shyly through the haze.

Jamie shifted slightly, their joined hands resting between them like something precious. He glanced down at her, his voice barely above a whisper.

"Can I—?"

Ellie turned to him, her heart fluttering against her ribs. She nodded once, the smallest motion, but sure.

He leaned in slowly, giving her every chance to pull away.

She didn't.

The kiss was soft — more breath than pressure, more question than answer. But it felt like the beginning of something she hadn't dared believe in.

When they pulled apart, neither of them spoke. They didn't need to.

Ellie didn't know what came next.

But for the first time in a long time, she wasn't afraid to find out.

8 SOMETHING LIKE LOVE

They never marked the day it began — not exactly.

There was no singular moment, no candlelit confession or sudden kiss beneath a bleeding sunset. It was quieter than that. More gradual. Like ivy growing up a wall — imperceptible at first, until one day, it was everywhere.

Jamie and Ellie fell in love the way some people find religion.

Wholly.
Unexpectedly.
With reverence.

The days grew longer, warmer. The courtyard exploded with life — green tangled with wildflower color, bees humming softly like distant applause. Ellie found herself waking earlier, not with dread, but with a kind of quiet anticipation.

She would open her window just to hear the faint murmur of Jamie's guitar drifting down the hall. It wasn't always beautiful. Sometimes it was clumsy or too loud or interrupted halfway by a curse. But it was *his*, and it filled the silence in her chest like light through stained glass.

One morning, he knocked on her door holding two coffees and a dog-eared copy of Neruda's *Twenty Love Poems*. He read to her in the courtyard, his voice barely above a whisper. Ellie didn't speak. She just closed her eyes and let the words crawl under her skin and live there.

They spent whole afternoons painting in silence, sketching and writing side by side, music playing low between them — Billie Holiday, Leonard Cohen, a little Nina Simone on sadder days. Sometimes Jamie would sing along without realizing it, and Ellie would pause, heart stilled, just to watch his mouth form words he didn't mean to share.

She read him poems she thought she'd forgotten. He told her stories he never meant to tell. They touched only sometimes — his hand brushing hers as he passed her a pencil, or her knee nudging his beneath the table. But the air between them always felt charged, like even their silences were intimate.

He made her laugh. Not the brittle, hollow kind she'd perfected with Mark — but loud, surprised laughter that made her clutch her stomach and feel, for a second, twenty again.

And she made him *still*. Grounded. Present. He told her once, in a rare moment of self-disclosure, that his whole life had felt like static until her. Like tuning a radio, always half-a-beat off, until her voice came through and he finally heard the music clearly.

They cooked together in her tiny kitchen — Jamie always improvising, Ellie reading the recipe out loud just to annoy him. They burned things, got drunk on red wine and jazz, and danced barefoot on hardwood floors until the room spun.

One night, after the dishes were stacked and the laughter had quieted, they lay on the couch, tangled in the warmth of red wine and music and something that felt dangerously close to forever.

There was no grand gesture. No carefully orchestrated moment.

Just a look — long and unguarded.

Just a breath — shared and held.

Jamie brushed a strand of hair from her cheek, his hand lingering there, and Ellie leaned into it like it was the most natural thing in the world.

When they kissed this time, it wasn't tentative.

It was real. Anchored. Full of everything they hadn't said but had always known.

Later, as they lay together in her bed, Ellie rested her head on his chest and listened to the rhythm of his heartbeat — steady, unwavering.

For once, she didn't feel like she had to protect herself.

For once, she let herself be held.

And she let herself believe that maybe love could be both wild and safe.

They watched thunderstorms from her window and played each other songs they swore the other *had* to hear. They left each other notes tucked into sketchbooks and mugs. Ellie still had one she particularly treasured — a quick pencil drawing of her sleeping on the couch, hair wild, mouth slightly open. Underneath, Jamie had written *You're even beautiful when you snore.*

Sometimes she caught him looking at her like she was art. Not pretty. Not flattering.

Important.

And sometimes, she looked at him and felt a fear so sharp it almost tasted metallic. Because loving Jamie was starting to feel like being alive in a way that scared her. He didn't *complete* her — he *saw* her. And that, somehow, was harder to accept.

One late night, after too much wine and a lasagna they both swore wasn't *that* burned, Jamie had followed her down the narrow hallway, laughing, barefoot, glowing.

"Wait," Ellie said, stopping near the end of the hall. She pointed toward a section of exposed brick above the old radiator. "There's a little hollow up there. I noticed it when I was painting."

Jamie leaned in, curious. "What kind of hollow?"

She stepped carefully onto the radiator — the metal warm beneath her feet from the last exhale of steam — and reached high to touch the edge of the brick wall.

"Right here. If you look closely, there's a little dip in the mortar line. Deep enough to tuck something in."

Jamie squinted up. "That's where I'd hide a love letter."

Ellie smiled but said nothing.

She stepped down slowly, her hand lingering on the wall.

Later, when everything had changed, she would return to this spot. When the words she couldn't speak became the only ones she could leave behind.

They loved each other like people who had forgotten how, and were remembering together.

It was not always easy. They fought sometimes — over nothing, or over everything. Jamie could be moody, and Ellie could retreat when things got too real. But every argument ended with some tender gesture — an apology scribbled on a napkin, a hand outstretched in the middle of the night, a whispered "Don't go."

The ivy in the courtyard had grown thick and wild. It framed the fountain like a crown, alive and reaching, as if echoing what had bloomed between them.

And still — in the quiet moments, when the air was too still or the night too dark — Ellie would feel the tremor of doubt.

What if this didn't last?

What if she was wrong again?

What if *she* broke it?

She told herself not to sabotage it. Not this time.

But deep inside, in a place untouched even by Jamie's softness, Ellie still feared the cost of being known. Of being loved when she wasn't sure she deserved it.

She tried to stay in the moment. She *wanted* to believe it could last.

But every time Jamie looked at her like she was his forever...a small voice inside whispered,

"Don't let him get too close. You know how this ends."

And that — *that* —is when fear slipped in through the door love had left open.

9 THE WEIGHT OF FOREVER

Jamie had always been expressive in the ways that didn't announce themselves.

The way he touched her lower back as he passed behind her in the kitchen.
The way he looked up from sketching, eyes lighting up like she was the sun he forgot he needed.
The way he kept her tea mug full without being asked, and read her poems in the quiet hours between midnight and morning.

But somewhere along the way, *love* had become unspoken only in name.

It was in every shared silence.
Every second glance.
Every night she fell asleep to the sound of his heartbeat pressed against her shoulder blade.

Jamie had fallen for her completely, unreservedly — a man not interested in half measures. His love was full and generous, without caution or exit strategy. He didn't fear what he felt. He didn't edit it.

And that was what made it so terrifying.

Ellie loved him too.

In a way she never had before — not even in the frantic, hopeful years of youth when love had been confused with being needed.

With Jamie, it was different.

It was calm and storm, comfort and ache.

He made her feel like she had come home to a version of herself she'd almost forgotten. He didn't try to fix her or mold her or wait for her to be easier to love. He simply *stayed* — constant, patient, with eyes that didn't look away when she turned brittle.

But the more certain he became, the more her fear expanded — silent and invasive, like smoke beneath a door.

It started with small things.

An offhand comment about forever.
A lingering glance, the kind that held more than he said out loud.

A missed call that sent her into a tailspin of wondering where he'd been.

Jamie was always where he said he'd be. Always honest, always present.
But *trust* wasn't built in real-time — not when your past had taught you that love, once certain, always became conditional.

Her scars weren't visible. But they were mapped across her heart like old burn marks.

Mark had once said he loved her too.

He had once promised forever.
And she had believed him.

34

So what if Jamie meant it *now*?
What about five years from now?
What about when she got older, when the thrill wore off, when someone younger or simpler or less *damaged* walked by?

She tried to ignore it.
Tried to laugh and kiss him and fold herself into the life they were building like it didn't feel too good to be true.

But anxiety doesn't ask permission.
It simply seeps in, quietly rearranging your mind until safety starts to feel like a trick.

And then, one afternoon in late August, as they sat in the courtyard eating peaches from a brown paper bag, juice dripping down their wrists, Jamie looked at her like she was the only thing keeping the sky from falling.

"I'm in love with you," he said, without ceremony. "I've never been more sure of anything in my life."

Ellie froze, heart catching on his words.
Six months, she thought. *It's only been six months.*
Too soon for forever. Too fast for certainty.
But God, she wanted to believe him.

He didn't stop.

"You're it for me, El. You're my person. I've waited a long time to find someone who *sees* me. And I see you. All of you. I don't want this to be temporary. I want it all. I want *you*."

He smiled, nervous but steady.

"I don't know what it'll look like — but I know I want to build a life with you. Maybe not now, not tomorrow. But someday. I want the whole thing. House keys. Morning breath. Growing old and strange together. All of it."

He said it like a gift.

But Ellie heard it like a clock ticking.

She smiled — or tried to — but something inside her had already begun to splinter.

That night, after he fell asleep beside her, his body warm and familiar, Ellie lay awake staring at the ceiling, her pulse thudding against her ribs like it was trying to escape.

Jamie's words circled her mind like birds in a burning sky.

"You're it for me."

What if she couldn't live up to that?

What if he loved her now because he didn't know what she'd become under pressure?

What if, one day, he woke up and saw the truth — that she was complicated, moody, haunted by doubts she didn't know how to silence?

What if he *left*?

Or worse — what if he *stayed* but stopped loving her?

Over the following weeks, the spiral gathered speed.

She began pulling away in microscopic ways.

Turning her face from kisses.

Avoiding eye contact during quiet mornings.
Laughing too hard at things that didn't deserve it.
Staying out just a little longer when she went to the store.

Jamie noticed, of course.

Asked once, softly, "Are you okay?"

She nodded too quickly. "Just tired."

He didn't push.

That was the worst part — he gave her space, which only made her
feel more ashamed of how much she needed to run.

She started thinking in "when" instead of "if."

When it fell apart.
When she disappointed him.
When he cheated.
When he left.

Better to leave first than be left.
Better to disappear while he still looked at her with love instead of
regret.

Better to carry the ache now than risk a deeper wound later.

She would write the letter soon.

She didn't know exactly what it would say yet, or if she'd even give
it to him.
Only that it would be the hardest thing she'd ever written.

And that it would be the only way to tell the truth without watching it
break his heart in real time.

---

10 SHE'S GONE

She was gone by the time the light hit the west wall.

Jamie stood in his kitchen, barefoot, holding the chipped blue mug with the tiny bird on the handle — the one she always reached for when she came over.

The apartment was quiet, but not empty.
Her absence was loud in all the little things she hadn't meant to leave behind:
A scarf, still draped over the back of his chair.
A pair of reading glasses on the windowsill, catching the late morning sun.
A note taped inside the cabinet in her looping handwriting:
Don't forget to buy lemons.

He hadn't seen her slip away, hadn't heard the door.
But when he woke and found her side of the bed empty, he told himself she'd just stepped out.
He waited. Made tea. Poured hers, too.
Just in case.

It was only when he opened the drawer by the door that it sank in.
Her key.
She'd left it — tucked in a folded napkin, like something delicate.
Final.

Then came the voicemail.
Thirty seconds. No goodbye. Just a soft, breaking voice saying:
"Don't worry. I'm okay. I just... I can't."

She hadn't left a letter.
Just... silence.
And the ghost of everything that had felt like home.

He walked into the living room, where her presence still lived in the edges —a blanket she'd always pulled over her lap, a stack of books she'd half-finished.
The canvas he'd propped up in the corner sat untouched, the paint dry, the colors muted.
He picked up the brush.
Set it down again.
He didn't know how to paint grief.
Not this kind.

Outside, the city went on — oblivious, indifferent.
A car horn.
A dog barking.
Someone arguing into a phone on the street below.
Life, in all its mundane cruelty, continued.

He walked to the bedroom.
Sat at the edge of the unmade bed where she had curled beside him only nights before.
The sheets no longer held her warmth, but her perfume — soft, herbal, grounding — still lingered faintly on the pillow.

He bowed forward, elbows on knees, hands clasped together like prayer.

They weren't kids.

This wasn't some wild infatuation.
They had lived.
They had earned their tenderness.

And because of that, he'd believed — God, he had believed —
that they were different.
That they'd hold on harder.
Love smarter.
Refuse to run.

But she had.
Not in anger.
Not in flames.
Just… quietly.
Like the chapter had ended while he was still mid-sentence.
Like the love had expired — or worse, had never been fully claimed.

But he knew better.
He knew how she looked at him when she thought he wasn't paying
attention — those quiet, reverent glances like he was something rare.
He knew how her breath hitched when she was happy but scared.
He knew how tightly she had held him in sleep, like she was afraid
of waking up alone.

She hadn't stopped loving him.
He was sure of that.

She had just stopped believing she could be loved that much without
being left.

Jamie lay back on the bed and stared up at the ceiling.
A thin crack spidered across the plaster, sharp and deliberate,
like something splitting slowly apart.

He had no idea what to do now.
No plan. No fix.

Only this:

He would paint her.
He would paint her until the silence made sense.
He would paint her everywhere.

11 THE LETTER

Ellie sat on the edge of Jamie's bed for a long time after he fell
asleep.
His breathing was deep, steady, one arm flung across her waist.
She gently moved it, careful not to wake him.
She pressed a kiss to his shoulder.
One last time.

It wasn't that she didn't love him.
That was the problem.
She loved him in a way that frightened her — too much, too deep.
The kind of love that stripped her bare, left no room to hide. And
Ellie had spent a lifetime building walls she didn't know how to live
without.

Jamie saw through them. He saw all of her — the mess, the doubt,
the quiet ache she carried like a second spine — and he loved her
anyway.

That kind of love was too big.
Too real.
And she didn't trust herself not to ruin it.

So she did the only thing she knew how to do.
She left before he could stop her.

Not because she didn't want him.

But because losing him — someday, somehow — would've destroyed her.

And running felt like the only kind of survival she still understood.

The hardwood floor was cool beneath her feet as she stood.
She gathered her clothes silently from the chair, stepping into them like muscle memory.
She didn't rush.
There was nothing frantic about this goodbye.
It was quiet. Necessary.

In the bathroom, she pulled her hair back and looked at herself in the mirror.
Her reflection looked older than she felt.
But also stronger.

Back in the kitchen, she washed the mug she had used that evening — the chipped blue one with the tiny bird on the handle — and set it carefully beside the sink.
She hesitated before opening the drawer by the door.
Her key was still on the ring.
She removed it and wrapped it in a linen napkin from the drawer, then set it gently inside.

She considered leaving a note.
But what would she say that wouldn't make it harder?

Instead, she reached for her phone.
Her hand shook as she hit "record."
Her voice barely made it above a whisper.

"Don't worry. I'm okay. I just... I can't."

She pressed send.

Ellie didn't go straight home.

She walked the city streets as the sky began to fade from indigo to gray.
Head down, hands in pockets, moving without direction.
Only when the chill began to bite through her coat did she turn toward her own apartment.

Inside, everything was still. Unchanged.
The books on the shelf.
The blanket folded at the foot of the bed.
The half-finished watercolor on her desk.
It didn't feel like coming home.

She opened the closet and pulled down the box she had once told herself she'd only open if she ever had to leave for real.
A scarf she'd knitted for Jamie last winter.
A small Polaroid of them laughing in the kitchen, flour on their faces.
And a folded sheet of cream stationery.

She sat down at her desk, turned on the lamp, and began to write.

She didn't address it.

Didn't sign it.

It wasn't a letter for him to read. She just needed to write it — for herself.
A quiet kind of closure, tucked away like a ritual..

She padded down the hallway barefoot, like a ghost.

She stopped at the radiator.
Stepped up slowly.
Her fingers found the hollow without searching.

She slid the letter inside.

Paused.
Breathed in the warmth rising from the radiator.
Ran her hand along the brick.
Then she stepped down, barefoot and steady.
Turned.

And walked away.

Over the next two weeks, Ellie slipped in and out of her apartment at
odd hours — early mornings, mid-afternoons, whenever she was sure
Jamie wouldn't be home.
She moved quickly, carefully.
No big boxes. No goodbyes.
Just quiet withdrawals — a coat from the closet, a book from the
shelf, the painting she'd once hung above the radiator.

It had been a whirlwind, those six months.
Fast and consuming, like falling in love on a moving train.
They'd laughed, cooked, stayed up too late talking about everything
and nothing.
And now it was over.
Not with a fight, but with distance.
A soft unraveling.

She didn't know where she was going, not exactly.
The storage unit had room for her things.
A girlfriend — someone she hadn't seen much of lately — offered
her a couch and a bottle of wine and a place to land until she figured
it out.

Ellie accepted with quiet gratitude.
No explanations. No breakdowns.
Just the words: *"It didn't work out."*

And that was enough.

12 SOMEONE WORTH REMEMBERING

It started with the eyes.

He didn't sketch them first. Didn't plan proportions or palette. He just stood in front of the wall — raw brick, sun-warmed and flaking — and lifted a brush.

He hadn't painted since she left.

It was stupid, probably. Painting a woman who wasn't coming back. On the side of a building she used to walk past on her way to the corner store. But the grief had to go somewhere, and this wall had been empty for too long.

Maybe she'd see it, maybe she'd sense his pain. Maybe she would come back to him.

He dipped the brush in deep gray and began with the irises — wide, knowing, and impossibly sad. They were exactly as he remembered them. She used to look at him like that when she thought he was saying something important. Or when he wasn't saying anything at all.

The first day, he only painted the eyes. He didn't even notice when his hand started to ache, or when his neck stiffened from looking up for so long. When he stepped back, the city was turning pink with dusk.

The eyes followed him.

The second day, he returned with more paint and a ladder. He filled in the curve of her jaw, the soft shadows under her cheekbones, the unruly waves of hair. She looked younger than she had in life — not out of revision, but memory. He painted her like she looked when she laughed mid-sentence, when the wind tugged at her coat, when she turned to him like he was the only person in the world.

Passersby slowed as the mural took shape. Some nodded. A few stopped to take photos. One woman asked who she was.

Jamie just said, *"Someone worth remembering."*

He didn't sign the mural. It wasn't about that.

It wasn't about being seen.

It was about *seeing her* — the version of her no one else had, the one who'd whispered poems under her breath, who had loved him in ways too deep to explain but not deep enough, apparently, to stay.

Jamie stepped back.

She looked out from the brick like she was waiting for something. Or someone.

Maybe she still was.

13 DEAR ELLIE

He tried.

Tried to date someone new. A woman named Clara who taught literature at the community college and liked old French films and winter hikes. She was kind. Smart. Beautiful, even — in a composed, careful way.

But she didn't make him forget.

He sat across from Clara at a cafe one rainy afternoon, nodding along as she talked about *The Lover* by Marguerite Duras, and realized he hadn't heard a word she'd said. His mind had wandered back to a Sunday with Ellie — the way she used to underline whole pages of books and then get mad at herself for doing it. *"It's like I'm vandalizing my own thoughts,"* she once said, laughing as she flipped through a dog-eared copy of *The Bell Jar*.

That was the moment he knew he wasn't ready.

Maybe he never would be.

That night, he found himself at the kitchen table, the one they used to sit at together, and pulled out an old notebook. He didn't plan to write her — the rational part of him knew there was no point. But the part of him that still checked the door some nights needed to say something.

He turned to a clean page and wrote her name at the top, like it might summon her.

Dear Ellie,

Then, he let it pour.

Jamie stepped into the courtyard, the late afternoon light slanting across the worn stone path. He made his way to the low wall where they used to sit — where laughter once echoed and secrets were whispered like confessions to the ivy.

He reached into his jacket pocket and pulled out the letter.

Ellie had once shown him the hollow behind a brick in her apartment wall — a tiny hidden space just big enough to tuck something private away. He had smiled then and said, "That's where I'd hide a love letter."

So instead, he found a similar hollow, loose and weathered, in the courtyard wall — their place. And with a hand that trembled slightly, he slipped the letter behind the brick.

A small act of goodbye. Or maybe hope. He wasn't sure which.

14 THE YEARS BETWEEN

Twenty years had passed.

Not all at once — not like the sweeping montages in movies where seasons blur and hair grays gracefully.

No, time had passed in dishes washed and dried. In bills paid. In quiet holidays. In strangers' laughter overheard at restaurants and long drives home in silence. In slow mornings and slower goodbyes. In birthdays and funerals and mail piling up by the door.

And still — somewhere beneath it all — Ellie and Jamie carried each other.

Jamie lived by the water now.

Not far — just a small coastal town where tourists came in the summer and left again in September. He had a studio with high ceilings and a skylight that leaked when it rained. The walls were covered in portraits. Not all of them were Ellie. But most of them were.

He painted less now. Or maybe just slower. Deliberately.

In the years since she left, Jamie had tried to move on. He dated — loved, even. Briefly married a woman named Rose who was gentle and patient and never asked about the sketch he kept in a drawer.

But no one filled the space Ellie left behind.

She had never belonged to him, not really.
But what they had — those six months — had imprinted on him like a fingerprint pressed into wet cement.

He had stopped hoping she'd return.
But he never stopped wondering what she'd look like now.
If she was okay.
If she thought of him.

Some nights, when the wind was just right, he thought he could still hear her voice — laughing low over bad coffee, reading Neruda like scripture.

He missed her like a missing verse in a song — always humming under the surface, incomplete.

Ellie had built a quiet life.
She never remarried.

She taught poetry workshops. Published two more books. Moved into a home with wide windows and a garden that grew wild no matter how much she tried to tame it.

There were people — men who came and went, friends who stayed longer. There was a woman once, tender and kind, who held her grief like it was something sacred.

But Ellie never let anyone too far in.

Not in the way Jamie had gotten in.

Not in the way that made her want to memorize the shape of a hand or whisper secrets into a cracked ceiling or keep a chipped blue mug by the sink just because someone liked it.

In the years since she left, Ellie had written dozens of poems she
never published — all about things she couldn't name. Memory.
Distance. The ache of almost.

She told herself she had made the right choice.
That it was better to leave while it was beautiful.
Better than waiting for the cracks to spread.
Better than breaking in front of someone who truly saw her.

But still, there were nights when she looked out at the moon and
whispered, "I'm sorry," to no one.

She didn't know if he'd moved on.
Didn't know if he hated her or pitied her or never thought of her
again.

But she still kept the drawing he'd once done of her — folded
between the pages of a book she never lent out.
And she still dreamt of him.
Not as he was.
As he had been, in the courtyard, in the quiet.

Now, at nearly seventy, Ellie needed help.

The tremors had started in her hands a few years ago. The
forgetfulness came later — slowly at first, then all at once. Her
doctor used words like *neurological decline* and *early-stage* and
supportive care. Eventually, the decision was made for her: she
moved into Bellwood Haven — a long-term residence not far from
the place where everything had begun.

Her world had become smaller.

Her days quieter.

But sometimes, she still wandered the garden at Bellhaven when no one was watching — drawn to it like a tide pulled by something older than memory.

She didn't remember everything.

But she remembered him.

They had survived the years.

They had grown older.

They had carried new joys, new hurts, new routines.

But beneath all of it, there was something unfinished — a thread left untied, a door quietly closed but never locked.

And neither of them knew it yet, but it was about to open again.

Because miles away, in a sunlit apartment filled with ivy and echoes, a young woman named Maisie had just found a letter hidden behind a loose brick above the radiator.

A letter that began,

Dear Jamie,

I don't know if you'll ever read this....

15 APARTMENT 4B
2025

Maisie didn't like the color of the walls.

They were a tired off-white, the kind that might once have passed for cream, before the city's years had dulled it to something between resignation and beige. Carter called it "timeless." Maisie called it tired.

The apartment was technically perfect — a high-ceilinged, sunlit corner unit in Manhattan's East Village with original crown molding and exposed brick. There was even a vintage record player in the corner when they toured it, and a reclaimed mid century modern wood coffee table that looked like it came with its own Instagram filter. It was one of those places people envied on social media, full of good angles and better lighting. Carter had fallen in love with it the moment they walked in. "It's a statement," he'd said, all crisp smiles and real estate bravado. "This place says something about who we are."

Maisie had nodded then, dazzled by his certainty, by the way he always seemed so sure of what they needed next.

In that moment, she let herself believe it was their dream home, too. She could still picture them laughing in the empty living room, barefoot on the paint-splattered drop cloth, takeout containers scattered like memories waiting to be unpacked. Carter had pulled her close, dancing with her to "True" by Spandau Ballet playing softly from his phone. They swayed together, lost in a world that, at least for a brief while, felt like it might actually belong to them.

They had met at a gallery opening in Chelsea six years ago — Carter in a tailored navy suit that somehow made him look both expensive and effortless, and Maisie in boots that pinched her toes but gave her the kind of posture that passed for confidence.

Maisie had just turned thirty back then — still soft-edged from her twenties, still open in a way she didn't realize was rare. She had the kind of beauty that snuck up on you — quiet, unpolished, the kind that made people turn for a second look without knowing why. Carter, three years older, had the sharp kind of presence that made people notice him instantly. He looked like a magazine ad for a lifestyle no one really lived — crisp collars, artfully tousled hair, and a watch that cost more than her rent.

He was debating the merit of a minimalist installation — a single cracked mirror hanging from fishing wire — when she cut in with, "It's just pretending to be broken. Like half the people in this room." He laughed. She didn't smile. He asked her to coffee anyway.

One coffee became three. Then came rooftop bars and early morning walks through SoHo and a whirlwind romance stitched together by ambition, charm, and just enough mystery to keep her leaning in. Carter was magnetic in that way — all crafted spontaneity and clean lines — and Maisie, still soft from a breakup that had left her untethered, mistook momentum for meaning.

But now, that certainty shimmered like a mirage — beautiful from a distance, but never truly real.

Maisie stood barefoot again, this time alone, with a paintbrush in hand and a can of "Palladian Blue" balanced beside her. Carter was at a rooftop cocktail party with someone named Vaughn. Or Chase. Or something equally exhausting. He'd texted earlier: *You don't have to come if you're busy with the walls.*

She didn't respond.

She was thinking about the time he'd corrected her pronunciation of "mozzarella" in front of the waiter — not as a joke, but with a kind of smug pride, as if he were doing her a favor. How he'd once rearranged the bookshelf not by author or genre, but by color — "for the aesthetic," he'd said, standing back to admire his work while she stared at the chaos of broken series and mismatched stories. Or the night they ran into his college friends at a bar in Tribeca and he introduced her as "an old soul with a cool-girl edge," like she was a brand he'd workshopped. She remembered laughing then, playing along, but the words had settled under her skin like sand in a shoe.

There had been other moments, too. Quiet ones. Uneasy ones. Like the way he always seemed more interested in how things appeared than how they felt, as if beauty could be curated, connection arranged, intimacy achieved by design.
He knew how to light a room, how to angle a photograph, how to dress a life so it looked enviable from the outside.
But scratch the surface — just a little — and it all felt hollow. Meant for display, not for living.
He didn't ask how she was feeling after a hard day, but he'd notice if her dress didn't match the table setting.
He remembered the filter she used on Instagram, but not the name of her childhood dog.
It was all surface.
And Maisie — who once believed in the beauty of small, messy truths — was beginning to suffocate under the weight of looking perfect.

Little things. But they lingered.

Maisie stepped onto the old radiator to reach the top edge of the brick wall in the hallway. The metal was warm beneath her soles, heated from the radiator's last exhale of steam. She leaned in, pressing the brush into the mortar lines.

Clink.

She paused.

The brush had hit something — not rough, not wall. Solid. Hollow.

She stepped down, eyebrows drawn. One of the bricks sat just a little deeper than the others. Curious, she set the brush aside and reached out, pressing her fingers against the edge. It gave, slightly.

She grabbed a screwdriver from the nearby toolbox and gently pried the brick forward. It shifted with surprising ease, revealing a small recess behind it.

Inside was a folded piece of yellowing paper, tied with a faded green ribbon.

Maisie stared. The space was just large enough to fit a hand — and, apparently, a secret. Her heart beat faster. Carefully, she drew the letter out and sat down on the hallway floor, paint drying behind her, knees drawn up.

The paper was soft and thin, the ink faded but readable. A woman's handwriting, elegant but rushed.

She untied the ribbon and unfolded the page.

Dear Jamie,

I don't know if you'll ever read this.
Maybe I'll lose my nerve. Maybe I'll burn it like I did the others.
Maybe it'll stay tucked behind the loose brick — that little hollow you once said was perfect for a love letter.

But I need to say it — even if it's just to paper and dust.

You were never just Sunday mornings and whispered promises.
You were the ache I didn't know I was carrying until you touched it.
You were the silence between songs — the part that holds all the meaning.
You were home, long before you stepped through my door with your arms full and your heart wide open.

And I ruined it.

Not because I didn't love you —
But because I did.

Because I loved you so wholly, so fiercely, that it terrified me.
I couldn't imagine a world without you — and somehow, that made
me leave.
I know it's backward. I know it doesn't make sense. But loving you
opened up a part of me I didn't know how to protect.
And the thought of losing you broke me long before I ever walked
away.

So I ran. I let fear disguise itself as reason.
I let the world tell me what I should want, and who I should be —
and I let you go.

I always loved that old bookshop on the corner — the only place that
felt like mine in this whole city. I used to sit in the poetry section and
read until the light changed. Maybe I was always looking for
something I couldn't name.

I'm sorry I wasn't stronger.
I'm sorry I didn't fight harder.
And I'm sorry I didn't stay. I needed to know who I was when I
wasn't holding my breath — but the truth is, I let fear win.

And if you ever find this —
If time and wood and brick and breath somehow carry it to you —
Know that every step I took away from you was a lie.
And that I have loved you every single day since.

Love,
Ellie

Maisie didn't know how long she sat there.

The letter was short — just one page — but it felt like a lifetime
pressed between lines.

She folded it slowly, carefully, and slid the ribbon back into place.

And for the first time in weeks — maybe months — she felt something break open inside her.

Not confusion. Not restlessness. Not even pain.

Curiosity.

Real, honest, gut-deep curiosity.

She ran her fingers over the brick's edge one last time.

Then, with the letter pressed against her heart, she stood.

And started to wonder who Ellie had been — and what had happened to Jamie.

16 THE MAN BEHIND THE CURTAIN

Maisie didn't sleep that night. Not really.

She lay in bed beside Carter, the letter folded and tucked into the drawer of her nightstand, as if keeping it close could make its truth clearer. His back was to her, rising and falling in the even rhythm of someone with nothing on their mind but tomorrow. Meetings. Appearances. Plans. A silk eye mask rested over his face, the kind infused with hyaluronic acid or green tea or something equally self-important — another ritual in his endless pursuit of looking effortlessly perfect. Carter was always in costume — dressed for the role of the man he thought the world wanted him to be. Confident. Cultured. *Contrived.*

Her thoughts, by contrast, were anything but even. They moved in messy loops. Who was Ellie? What happened to Jamie? What kind of love made someone write something that raw and never send it? What kind of fear kept you from fighting for something that real?

She thought she knew fear. The fear of letting people down. Of making the wrong turn. Of ending up alone. But now, a quieter, deeper fear had settled into her chest — the fear of waking up one day and realizing she'd built a life that never really belonged to her. A life full of pretty things and perfect plans, but empty of anything that stirred her soul. And somehow, that felt more terrifying than loneliness ever could.

When sleep did come, it was fractured and thin, the kind that left her more tired when she woke up. The kind that followed you around like a fog.

Carter barely glanced at her over coffee the next morning.

"You used the wrong paint," he said casually, scrolling through his phone.

Maisie blinked. "What?"

He gestured toward the wall with his mug. "The tone. It clashes with the furniture. I sent you the swatches last week, remember?"

Maisie stared at him. "It's paint, Carter."

"It's *our* apartment, Maisie. Details matter."

Our. She swallowed her response and stood, putting her mug in the sink.

Carter was in luxury real estate — the kind of agent who didn't just sell homes, he sold lifestyles. He had a talent for making square footage feel like destiny, for turning exposed brick and brass fixtures into personality traits. Everything he touched became a projection — a stage set, perfectly lit and hollow underneath. His Instagram was a gallery of rooftop views, marble countertops, and client selfies with captions like *Another dream home matched.* He wore tailored suits to open houses and called apartments "spaces," and Maisie had once watched him spend ten full minutes adjusting a vase before a showing. He didn't just sell the dream — he believed in it, lived in it, needed it to be real. Even if, deep down, it never really was.

"I found something yesterday," she said, unsure why she was offering it, even as she spoke. "In the wall. A letter. From someone who lived here decades ago."

He barely looked up. "That's cool. Like a time capsule?"

Maisie hesitated. "More like… a love letter. From a woman named Ellie to someone named Jamie. It was hidden. Really hidden."

Carter looked at her now, but with a bemused smile. "You've always liked sentimental stuff."

She stared at him, trying to find something in his eyes — interest, curiosity, warmth, affection. Anything. But Carter's eyes, like his life, were polished surfaces. Reflective but impenetrable.It was the same look he gave her when she bought old postcards at flea markets. A kind of fond indulgence. Not connection.

Maisie worked as a freelance copywriter, mostly for small businesses and indie brands — makers of organic soap, handmade jewelry, vintage bookstores trying to stay relevant online. She liked the quiet rhythm of it, the challenge of finding the right words to make something feel honest. She worked mostly from home, often tucked into the corner of the living room with her laptop and a mug of cold coffee she kept forgetting to warm up. It didn't pay much, and Carter often referred to it as "a cute side hustle," which she found dismissive and belittling. For her, it was real work — creative, meaningful, and hers. But lately, even her words felt stuck, like they were waiting for her to be honest with herself first.

She spent the day pretending to be productive. She repotted a plant, deleted four unanswered emails from the wedding photographer, and tried to write thank-you notes for gifts they hadn't received yet. But her mind kept drifting.

To the letter.

To the ache in Ellie's words. To what it meant to love like that — so deeply it frightened you.

Maisie wondered if she had ever made Carter feel that way. If he had ever truly made *her* feel that way.

That evening, Carter texted her at 6:12 p.m.

Meet me at Folie. Reservation at 7. Just us.

It was their anniversary. Six years since their first date.

Carter proposed a year ago during a weekend getaway to the Amalfi Coast, on a balcony overlooking the sea, just as the sun dipped low enough to bathe everything in that golden light photographers chase. A private chef had just cleared the dessert plates when Carter dropped to one knee with a vintage ring he'd sourced from "a discreet Parisian dealer." A drone buzzed overhead, capturing the moment for the professionally edited video he'd later post with the caption *"She said yes"*. Maisie had smiled — of course she had — caught somewhere between the romance of it all and the strange, sinking feeling that the proposal had been designed more for the highlight reel than for her. It should have felt like coming home. Instead, it felt like stepping onto a stage.

She had forgotten. So had he, apparently — until his assistant reminded him.

Oh yes, his assistant…with legs for days, a permanent pout, and a voice that made every sentence sound like a question, even when she was stating obvious facts — like once asking if Vermont was "next to Europe." Maisie couldn't help but wonder if Carter had hired her for her résumé or her bustline — and which one he valued more.

Maisie changed quickly and walked the twelve blocks in heels that pinched and a dress she'd worn twice before because Carter liked the color.

Folie was sleek and candlelit, the kind of place where everything was plated in gold or microgreens. Carter was already seated at a corner table, sipping something expensive and checking his phone.

"You look great," he said, rising just enough to kiss her cheek without smudging his perfectly styled hair. His eyes swept over her dress like he was appraising a painting — appreciative, but distant. "I went ahead and ordered the octopus to start," he added, already flagging the waiter with a flick of his wrist, as if her preferences were a formality they'd long outgrown.

Maisie sat across from him and looked around. The room was full of beautiful people talking about real estate and private equity. People who, like Carter, seemed to exist more easily as impressions than individuals. She wondered what Jamie would have thought of a place like this. She wondered what Ellie would've written about it.

"Happy anniversary," Maisie said.

Carter raised his glass. A chilled Sancerre, of course — crisp, French, and just obscure enough to sound impressive when he said it. *"To us. To the future."*

She tapped her glass against his and took a sip. It had notes of citrus and flint, a hint of pear on the finish — and just the faintest trace of pretension, like it had been aged in an ego and bottled for show.

Halfway through dinner, he started talking about the venue.

"I was thinking we could book that string quartet you liked," Carter said, slicing into his steak. "The one from your Pinterest board."

Maisie blinked. "I haven't looked at that board in a year."

He shrugged. "Well, you used to care about that kind of thing."

She set her fork down. "Do you actually think you know me?"

Carter looked confused. "Of course I do. We've been together for six years."

"That's not what I asked." Maisie wasn't asking for facts. She was asking to be seen — and Carter didn't know the difference.

He stared at her for a moment, then leaned back. "Where is this coming from?"

Maisie looked down at her plate. "I don't know. Maybe I'm just tired."

Carter didn't press her. He just nodded, took a final sip of his wine, and glanced at his watch.

"Well, I've got that event at the gallery tonight," he said, his tone casual — like the whole exchange had been about the weather. Obviously, her words hadn't landed at all. "You can come, if you want."

Maisie shook her head. "I think I'll head home."

He stood, buttoned his jacket, and leaned in to kiss her cheek. "Try to get some rest, okay?"

And just like that, the moment passed.

Later that night, Carter came home late from a networking event, smelling of rooftop martinis and a cologne she didn't recognize. He kissed her on the cheek — quick, distracted — and handed her a glossy gift bag with a monogrammed robe folded neatly inside. "Figured it'd look good in the wedding prep photos," he said, already unbuttoning his shirt. "Everyone's doing those now." He didn't meet her eyes when he said it, and she noticed his phone screen light up twice before he turned it face down on the counter. Always another message. Another audience. Always something behind the curtain.

Maisie stared at the robe.

It was ivory. Satin. Her new initials embroidered in gold.

It felt like a costume for someone else's life. And Carter, the man behind the curtain, was just playing his part.

"Thanks," she said quietly, folding it neatly and placing it on the chair.

Carter didn't notice. He was already in the bathroom, brushing his teeth while replying to emails.

Maisie curled up under the blanket, the letter tucked beneath her pillow, and let her eyes drift closed.
She imagined Ellie standing there, heart full and trembling, choosing to walk away — not out of certainty, but out of fear disguised as wisdom.

She imagined Jamie waiting, day after day, for words that never arrived.

And she wondered how long it took before he stopped hoping. The thought stayed with her, quiet and steady.

Maisie didn't want a life that looked perfect from the outside.

She wanted one that felt like hers.

17 THE IVY KEPT GROWING ANYWAY

Maisie didn't tell Carter where she was going.
Not because she was hiding — not exactly.
But because she was tired of justifying anything that didn't align with his idea of useful.
The bookstore wasn't on a schedule. It wasn't productive, impressive, or particularly photogenic.
It was quiet. Dusty. Full of forgotten things and unsaid thoughts.
And lately, Maisie had started craving the kind of quiet Carter would dismiss as a waste of time.

So she slipped out quietly, letting the door close behind her without a word. It was a Tuesday morning, unusually warm for early spring, and she walked two avenues east with the letter folded carefully inside her journal. Her steps were purposeful, even if she wasn't entirely sure what she hoped to find. *"I always loved that old bookshop on the corner — the only place that felt like mine in this whole city."* There was only one place that made sense to start: the secondhand bookstore three blocks away. The woman who owned it — gray hair in a tight braid, sweater that smelled like cedarwood — had helped her before when she'd been looking for a rare wedding poem Carter had wanted framed.

Back then, the owner had offered a polite smile — the kind reserved for casual customers. Today, Maisie needed more than small talk.

The bell above the door jingled as she stepped inside. The air smelled like aged paper and something sweetly nostalgic. Sunlight filtered through high, dusty windows and bathed the space in quiet gold.

The woman looked up from behind the counter, perched on a stool like she'd been carved into it. "Back again," she said. Maisie was surprised that she had remembered her.

Maisie pulled the letter from her journal and set it gently on the counter. "I found this letter hidden in the wall of our apartment. I think it's from a long time ago. Do you recognize the name Ellie?"

The woman leaned in, adjusted her glasses, and read.

She didn't speak for a long time.

Finally, she said, "There was an Ellie Hart. She wrote the most beautiful poetry. She used to do readings at the community co-op on 14th. Quiet. Thoughtful. Had this way of writing about heartbreak that felt... personal"

Maisie's heart skipped. "Do you know what happened to her?"

The woman shook her head. "She disappeared about 20 years ago. Just like that. Some said she ran off with a lover. Others said she went home to care for a sick parent. Nobody ever really knew."

Maisie tucked her hair behind her ear. "Was there a Jamie?"

The woman's expression shifted. "Jamie Reed. He lived in that building too, I think. Jamie was an artist," she said. "He painted that mural on the side of the old brick building off 14th — the one with Ellie's face staring out like a ghost. Everyone knew it was her."

Maisie exhaled. "Did they end up together?"

The woman tilted her head, a soft smile playing at the corners of her mouth. "Some stories don't end so much as they drift," she said.

"They loved each other, that much was clear. But whether that love found a landing place… I suppose that's the part no one ever really knew."

She disappeared into a back room and returned a few minutes later with a small stack of chapbooks — self-published collections with names like *Beneath the Ivy* and *Where Dust Settles*. The covers were faded, edges worn, the kind of fragile books no one buys but no one throws away.

"Some of her work," the woman said. "If you want to read more."

Maisie nodded gratefully, cradling the stack like treasure, and left.

Maisie hadn't meant to walk that way. She'd left the book store with every intention of taking her usual route home — the one that passed the florist with the crooked awning and the antique shop she never entered but liked knowing was there. But something pulled at her, a gentle nudge just beneath reason, and she found herself turning down 14th instead.

The old brick building came into view slowly, like a memory returning. And then she saw it — the mural.

It stretched across the side of the building like a secret whispered in color. The paint was weathered but still vivid, a kaleidoscope of deep blues and sun-warmed golds. At the heart of it was the face of a woman, rendered with such aching tenderness that Maisie felt her breath catch. The woman's features were soft, luminous, alive in a way that seemed impossible on crumbling brick.

But it was the eyes that held her there.

There was something in them — something wide and knowing and impossibly sad. A quiet kind of longing, like the woman had waited a lifetime to be seen. And in that gaze, Maisie felt an echo of herself. Not the polished version she showed the world, but the one who still dreamed in the quiet hours, who still hoped for something more.

She stood there for a long time, the city moving around her, unnoticed. It wasn't just art on a wall. It was a message — a fragment of love, of loss, of truth left behind. And somehow, it made her feel less alone.

Like someone, once, had known exactly what it meant to be afraid of wanting too much — and walked away before it could be taken from her.

She spent the rest of the day at her kitchen table, sunlight shifting across the floor, coffee going cold beside her. She read every poem slowly, then again. The writing was unmistakably Ellie's — soft, sad, brimming with yearning.

One poem in particular made her pause:

I left the window open but you never knocked.
The ivy kept growing anyway.

The final page of one book had a faint scribble in pencil:

To J — You always saw me. Even when I couldn't.

Maisie traced her finger over the words.

Saw me.

She hadn't felt seen in a long time.

Later that evening, restless and needing air, Maisie wandered into the courtyard behind the building. The ivy-covered walls looked tired from winter, the garden beds mostly bare but quietly waiting. She paused, eyes tracing the stubborn green climbing the brick, and the line from Ellie's poem rose in her mind, soft and steady: *The ivy kept growing anyway.* A few chairs sat crooked on the stone patio, and the smell of damp soil and rust clung to everything.

"Don't mind the mess," a voice called out from behind a bush. "Spring makes fools of us all."

Maisie turned.

A man in a denim jacket and work boots stood up, wiping his hands on his jeans. He looked to be in his early thirties — around Maisie's age — with tousled dark hair, strong shoulders, and a beard that looked more like a natural feature than a fashion statement. His jaw was square, his smile a little lopsided, and his eyes — a deep, stormy gray — held an easy steadiness. There was something undeniably handsome about him, but unpolished in a way that made it feel honest. He looked like the kind of man who could fix a leaky faucet and build a fire without YouTube.

"I'm Rex," he said, nodding toward the garden. "Super's son. I help out down here when my dad's back acts up, which is… often."

Maisie smiled. "Maisie. We just moved in. Apartment 4B." She glanced over her shoulder, then back at him. "I had to get out for a bit — the paint fumes were starting to get to me."

Rex raised his brows. "4B? That used to be Ellie Hart's place. A few people have come and gone since, but none of them made much of an impression. She did. I was just a kid when she left, but I remember her."

Maisie paused. "Ellie Hart... you know that name?"

He shrugged, brushing dirt off his hands. "People still talk about her sometimes. My dad says she used to do readings out here, poetry and stuff. Said she had a voice that made you stop what you were doing — like the building itself was listening."

Maisie paused. She'd told the woman at the bookstore, yes — but that had felt different. Distant. Safe, in the way strangers behind counters can be. This was face-to-face. Real. And she wasn't sure why, but something in Rex's tone — the easy honesty of it — made her feel like she could say the thing she hadn't planned to.

She looked down at her shoes, then up at the old building behind him.

"I found something," she said, quieter than before. "A letter… in the wall. From her. To someone named Jamie."

Rex gave a low whistle. "No kidding. That's wild."

"It was folded up inside a loose brick behind the wall," she said. "She wrote about leaving. About loving someone and being scared. It felt... private. Like I shouldn't have read it, but I couldn't stop."

He studied her for a moment, head tilted. "Sometimes the things we're not meant to find are the ones meant for us most."

Maisie looked at him — really looked — and for a moment, the courtyard seemed quieter, like even the branches above were listening. There was something about Rex's presence — steady, unhurried — that settled into her like warmth.

They stood there in the silence, not awkward, just shared.

Then Rex nodded toward the far side of the courtyard. "There's a guy on the second floor, unit 2B. He's been here forever. Might know more about Ellie, if you're curious."

Maisie smiled, feeling something soft bloom in her chest. "Thank you."
Rex reached into the pocket of his jacket and pulled out a tiny sprig of lavender. "For your windowsill," he said, holding it out. "Smells better than fresh paint."

She took it carefully, their fingers brushing — a brief touch, but enough to stir something small and undeniable.

"See you around," he said.

Maisie watched him walk back toward the building, the scent of lavender rising in her hand like something remembered.

That night, Carter came home late again. He didn't notice the books on the table or the lavender in the jar. His shirt was half untucked, his smile a little too practiced. He kissed the top of her head, muttered something about investors, and disappeared into the shower — leaving the scent of unfamiliar perfume clinging faintly in the air behind him.

Maisie opened her journal and copied down the scribbled note from Ellie's book.

You always saw me. Even when I couldn't.

Then, underneath it, she wrote:

When did I stop being seen? Was I ever truly seen at all?

And for the first time, she began to realize that this wasn't just Ellie's story she was chasing.

It was her own.

18 TREASURE MAP

The next morning, Maisie stood at the kitchen window long after her tea had gone cold. Ellie's poetry books lay open on the table behind her, still marked with sticky notes and pencil underlines, Maisie's quiet way of dissecting a stranger's love story — and, somewhere along the way, unraveling her own.

Carter had left early. He had a breakfast meeting uptown with someone "important," and he'd paused only long enough to check his reflection and ask Maisie if she remembered to confirm their menu tasting appointment for Saturday.

"Sure," she'd said, though she hadn't. She wasn't even sure which caterer it was anymore.

Now, sunlight warmed the tile floor, and she couldn't stop rereading the note at the back of the final chapbook:
To J — You always saw me. Even when I couldn't.

Maisie stared at her reflection in the windowpane and whispered, "I want to be seen."

She tucked the books into her tote, grabbed her coat, and made her way down to the second floor. Rex had mentioned an older tenant who'd been there "forever." She knocked lightly, half hoping no one would answer.

But the door creaked open, revealing a man with thinning white hair, thick glasses, and a cardigan covered in paint smudges.

"Hi," Maisie said, her voice tentative. "I'm Maisie. I just moved in upstairs. I was wondering if you might remember someone — Ellie Hart?"

The man blinked slowly, then motioned for her to come in. "She was the one with the notebook," he said. "Always writing. Always watching. Quiet, but not shy. Jamie used to tell her she wrote the way artists dream of painting.

Maisie sat on a worn armchair. The apartment smelled like turpentine and old soup.

"I found a letter she wrote," she said. "To Jamie."

The man smiled wistfully. "They were something, those two. Didn't flaunt it, but you could feel it. Like heat between storm clouds. She left suddenly, though. Broke Jamie."

Maisie leaned forward. "Did she say why?"

He shrugged. "People didn't talk about feelings much back then. But he stayed for a while. Painted less. Smiled less. Then he left, too."

"Do you know where?"

"No clue. He didn't tell anyone. Just packed up his brushes and disappeared."

Maisie thanked him and left feeling both closer and further from the answers she wanted. She wandered out to the courtyard to think.

Rex was there again, kneeling beside a stubborn patch of earth near the old garden bed. The lavender plant he'd given her had been joined by a few other herbs and flowers, scraggly but surviving.

"You're making progress," she said.

He looked up and grinned. "This place needs a second chance."

"Don't we all," Maisie murmured.

Rex paused, his smile lingering but softening at the edges. There was something in her voice — not self-pity, not performance, just honesty, stripped bare. It made him want to know what she'd been through, what she was carrying that made those three words land like truth. He didn't push. But in that moment, he saw her differently — not just the woman from 4B, but someone trying, quietly, to grow something new from whatever had come before.

She sat on the low stone wall beside him, watching the wind play with the loose strands of her hair.

"I talked to someone in the building," she said. "He remembered Ellie and Jamie. Said they were in love. That she left and it wrecked him."

Rex wiped his hands on his jeans. "Sounds familiar."

Maisie tilted her head. "You've been through something like that?"

He didn't answer right away. "Let's just say I understand what it means to love someone who chooses not to choose you."

They sat in silence for a while.

"I don't know what I'm doing," Maisie admitted. "I'm supposed to be planning a wedding. Picking linen colors. But I can't stop thinking about this letter. About them."

Rex looked at her, not with judgment, but with a kind of quiet recognition. "Maybe you see yourself in her."

Maisie just nodded.

He paused, then reached into his pocket for a pen and tore a scrap from an old receipt. "My friend Lena volunteers at a senior residence upstate," he said, scribbling as he spoke. "She mentioned a woman there—used to be a poet, keeps to herself." He handed her the slip of paper, the ink still fresh.

Maisie stared at the paper. "Are you serious?"

"Could be nothing," Rex said. "Could be everything."

She clutched the slip like it might vanish. "Thank you."

Rex smiled. "You've got this look — like someone just handed you a treasure map."

"I think maybe you did."

19 BEFORE THE LEAP

The following morning, Maisie stood in the middle of the living room surrounded by swatches of silk, linen, and chiffon. They'd arrived in a tailored package from the wedding planner — a perfect little box of "touch and feel inspiration" that Carter had insisted would help them "visualize the day."

Maisie touched the smooth fabrics, then let her hand drop. None of them stirred anything inside her.

She picked up her phone and opened her gallery. Photos of flower arrangements. Tablescapes. Mock place settings. Then a picture she'd taken of Ellie's letter, tucked safely between pages of her notebook. The script, aged and aching, stared back at her with more meaning than any of the color palettes ever had.

By early afternoon, Maisie found herself back in the city, needing space from her own thoughts.

She ducked into a coffee shop near Union Square, a small place with creaky wooden floors and hand-painted mugs. She ordered a lavender latte — her new favorite — and pulled out her notebook.

The letter was folded neatly inside, now a bit softer at the edges from how often she handled it. She read it again, underlining a new sentence this time: *You were the ache I didn't know I was carrying until you touched it.*

She wondered if Ellie had ever told Jamie how she really felt — if there had ever been a confrontation, or if the letter was the only truth she ever allowed herself to speak.

Maisie looked up and noticed a couple at a nearby table. They were laughing — heads close, fingers touching. It wasn't the expensive kind of love. It wasn't manufactured. It was messy, unfiltered affection.

She sipped her drink and stared out the window, unsure whether she was mourning something she'd lost, or something she'd never had.

When she returned home, Carter was in the kitchen wearing an apron she didn't know they owned. He was chopping basil with alarming precision.

"Hey," he said brightly. "Thought I'd cook tonight. Pasta. From scratch. Figured we could have a cozy night in."

Maisie blinked. "Since when do you cook?"

He shrugged. "Saw it on a video. You've been stressed. I thought this might help."

She smiled, grateful for the gesture, but it landed awkwardly. Like a performance. Like he was reading from a script written for a different version of them.

They sat down to eat as the sky darkened outside. Carter lit candles, poured wine, made small talk about real estate trends and an influencer who'd booked their same wedding photographer.

Maisie tried to match his energy, but her thoughts kept drifting — to Ellie, to Jamie, to the quiet courtyard, to Rex.

Halfway through the meal, Carter paused mid-sentence and looked at her.

"You're somewhere else," he said.

Maisie set her fork down. "I've just got a lot on my mind."

"You've had a lot on your mind for weeks."

She nodded. "I know."

He reached across the table and took her hand. "I miss you."

Maisie looked at him. Really looked. His eyes were sincere. He was trying.

But she couldn't ignore the ache that bloomed in her chest — not from guilt, but from clarity.

"I miss me too," she said quietly.

After dinner, she slipped out into the courtyard for air—or at least, that's what she told herself. The truth was, she was hoping to see Rex. The night was cool, the air tinged with early spring dampness. The flowers were just beginning to wake up.

Rex was there, sitting on the low stone wall, a book open in his lap. He looked up as she approached.

"Escaping, too?" he asked with a grin.

She smiled faintly. "He's trying."

"And you?"

Maisie sat beside him, folding her hands in her lap. "I'm unraveling."

Rex nodded slowly. "That's not always a bad thing."

She tilted her head back and looked up at the stars barely visible above the buildings. "Did you ever stay with someone, even when you knew it wasn't right?"

Rex closed his book and set it aside. "Yeah. Sometimes you stay because part of you still hopes it'll turn into something it's not."

Maisie turned to look at him. "I found her. Ellie. Or at least, I think I did."

Rex looked up, quiet for a beat. "Bellwood Haven?"

She nodded. "Yeah. I called. They said there's a woman there— Eleanor Hart. Keeps to herself, writes sometimes. It has to be her."

Rex nodded slowly. "That's what Lena said. Ellie doesn't say much about the past."

"I want to go," Maisie said. "I think I need to."

"I'll drive," Rex offered, without hesitation.

Maisie stared at him — at the softness in his voice, the steadiness in his presence.

It made her want to cry and smile at the same time.

"Thank you," she said.

They sat together in the dark a while longer, saying nothing.

Maisie let the silence wrap around her like a wool coat — grounding, honest, real.

Not confusion. Not restlessness.

Just the deep breath before the leap.

20 REGRETS AND REVERIES

The drive to Bellwood Haven took three hours, but it felt like no time at all.

Maisie rode in silence for most of it, her forehead pressed to the cool window, watching the city dissolve into rolling hills and open sky. The farther they got from Manhattan, the easier it was to breathe.

Rex didn't try to fill the quiet. Occasionally, he'd glance over and offer her a small, reassuring smile. He played a mix of older records from his phone — soft, crackling vocals, acoustic guitars, lyrics that seemed to understand longing without explanation. *Neil Young's "Change Your Mind"* hummed low in the background, his voice full of weariness and truth: *"When you get weak, and you need to test your will… when life's complete, but there's something missing still…"* Then came *The Band*, their harmonies swelling like a sigh that had waited years to be exhaled: *"Now there's no love as true as the love that dies untold… but the clouds never hung so low before."* The music curled around them like candlelight — soft, searching, and just a little sad. Maisie was grateful for the quiet companionship. The kind that asked nothing. The kind that understood everything.

"This feels like something," she said finally, somewhere outside Albany.

Rex glanced at her. "Something scary or something good?"

Maisie smiled faintly. "Both."

They pulled up to Bellwood Haven just after noon. It wasn't what Maisie expected. Not a sterile facility or a hallway echoing with linoleum and wheelchairs, but something gentler — more like an old country estate. Wooden benches rested beneath sugar maples, and the flowerbeds spilled over with color, untamed but intentional — like someone had loved them without needing to control them.

Inside, an upright piano stood near the front window, and in the common room, two older women were playing chess while a man napped with a cat curled on his lap.

The receptionist, a young woman named Joy, greeted them with a kind smile. "Hi there. Who are you here to see?"

"Eleanor Hart," Maisie replied, her voice steadier than she expected. "If she's accepting visitors."

Joy glanced at the clipboard. "She's in the garden — usually heads out there after lunch. Doesn't love company, but she's always polite about it."

Maisie's heart thudded in her chest. "Thank you."

Outside, the garden was a peaceful spread of gravel paths, bird feeders, and aged stone fountains. Wind chimes clinked softly in the breeze. Near a koi pond sat a woman with long silver hair tied into a loose braid. She wore a denim jacket despite the warmth and had a leather-bound notebook in her lap. She was beautiful in that effortless, enviable way—cool without trying, like someone pretending she had it all figured out—and almost pulling it off.

Maisie walked slowly, her palms damp.

"Eleanor?"

The woman looked up. Her eyes were sharp and pale — not cold, but guarded. And in an instant, Maisie knew. They were the same eyes

83

from the mural, the ones that had followed her down 14th Street, full of something unspoken and impossible to forget. This was her. The woman Jamie had painted into brick and memory.

"Yes?"

Maisie hesitated. "My name is Maisie. I think... I think I live in your old apartment. I found something that belonged to you."

Ellie's gaze didn't change, but she closed her notebook. "What did you find?"

Maisie took a slow breath and pulled the folded letter from her coat pocket. She offered it gently. "This."

Ellie's expression softened. She took the letter, unfolded it slowly, and stared at the words in her own handwriting. She didn't speak for a long time.

Maisie sat down on the bench beside her, close but not too close. "I wasn't trying to intrude. I just... it changed something for me. Reading it."

Ellie nodded slowly, eyes still on the page. "I wrote this the night before I left."

Maisie studied her. "Why didn't you send it?"

Ellie folded the letter again, her fingers trembling. "Because I didn't trust it. Or myself. Jamie was... everything I didn't expect. Gentle, honest, all heart. But I'd just come out of something that wrecked me, and I didn't believe I could recognize real love anymore — let alone deserve it."

She looked away for a moment, then back at Maisie.

"And everyone around me thought I'd lost my mind. Falling for someone so deeply, so fast — at my age? I let their doubt become my own. I convinced myself it was a phase, a fantasy. That walking

84

away was the mature thing to do. But it wasn't. It was fear. I left because I was terrified that if I let myself want that kind of love… and it didn't last… it would break something in me I couldn't fix."

Maisie felt something tighten in her chest.

"I think I'm with someone who isn't Jamie," she admitted. "He fits the plan. But I don't think I do anymore."

Ellie met her eyes, a gentle understanding in her voice. "The heart doesn't get confused. It just waits for us to listen."

Maisie swallowed, the words settling in her chest like a truth she'd known all along.
"Then I guess I've been ignoring mine for a long time."

Ellie leaned back against the bench and looked out at the pond. "Let me tell you something about growing old. You stop worrying about whether something is easy or logical or convenient. You think about what you'd regret if the clock ran out tomorrow. That's it. That's the whole equation."

Maisie swallowed hard. "Do you regret it?"

Ellie nodded once. "Every day. Not because he was perfect, but because he made me feel real. I've had a good life. But never that kind of love again. I lost him. Not just emotionally. I mean… really lost him."

They sat in silence for a few moments, the birds chirping overhead.

"I didn't know what I was looking for when I found that letter," Maisie said. "But it's changed everything."

Ellie looked down at her lap. "Then maybe it did what it was meant to do."

She reached into her notebook and tore out a page. "This was for him. I never sent it either. Maybe it'll help."

Maisie accepted the paper carefully. It was a poem:

If I could do it over,
I'd stay in the room.
I'd speak the words.
I'd let the silence break me open.

Maisie blinked back tears. "Thank you."

Ellie smiled softly. "Go live something worth writing about."

When Maisie returned to the lobby, Rex was waiting, sipping coffee from a paper cup.

He stood when he saw her. "How'd it go?"

Maisie held up the poem like a piece of treasure. "She remembered everything."

Rex nodded. "You okay?"

Maisie let out a long, shaky breath. "I think I finally am."

She looked out the window toward the garden — toward a woman who once hid her truth behind a brick wall.

Maisie wouldn't do the same.

She was ready to break her own silence.

21 THE QUIET ONES

He'd always liked the quiet ones.
Not because they were easy, or soft, or passive — but because they listened. Not just to words, but to everything between them.

Maisie was one of those.

She sat in the courtyard like she belonged there, even though she still looked like she was trying to decide if she did. Some people move into a place, fill it with noise, and call it home. Maisie moved like she was asking permission first.

Rex noticed things — it came with the job. Loose pipes. Flickering bulbs. Tenants who needed space. Tenants who needed excuses to talk. Maisie didn't ask for anything, but she'd started showing up. Sitting on the stone wall. Letting her hands trail over the brick like it held answers.

He noticed the way her shoulders dropped when she was near him. The way her voice softened, like she didn't have to hold it up all the time. That meant something.

Rex wasn't good at grand gestures. He didn't come with champagne or speeches or rooftop parties. He came with spare keys and lavender sprigs and the ability to fix things that were broken. Not everything. But some things.

He'd seen a lot of couples in this building. The loud ones. The picture-perfect ones. The kind that posed well for the world and fell apart in the hallway. Maisie and Carter had that feel. Glossy. Tight-lipped.

When Carter passed him in the stairwell, he barely looked up.

When Maisie passed, she smiled. Even when it didn't reach her eyes.

Rex wasn't trying to fall for her. That kind of thing didn't happen in real life — not like it does in movies. But he found himself watching the windows more often. Hoping to see her light come on. Noticing when she wasn't around.

He didn't know what she needed.

But he hoped, when she figured it out, she'd let him be the one who gave it to her.

22 WHAT ARE THE ODDS?

She hadn't meant to sit there.
The courtyard garden had drawn her in again, the way it always did.
It was one of those bright, impossibly still afternoons where the
world seemed to hold its breath. A breeze moved through the flowers
like a whisper. Somewhere above her, a pigeon cooed without
urgency. The sun warmed the brick behind her back.

Maisie sat on the low stone wall, her fingers absentmindedly tracing
the grooves in the bricks beside her, as she often did. They were
uneven, time-worn. A few were chipped. One — just one — felt
different. It shifted slightly under the lightest pressure of her hand.

She stilled.

A strange feeling swept through her — part memory, part intuition.
As if she'd been here before.
As if something *wanted* her to look.
She didn't believe in signs. Not really. But in that moment, it felt like
the universe had paused just long enough for her to notice something
she was always meant to find.

She pressed again. A slow, cautious nudge. The brick gave a little.

Her heart began to pound.

It couldn't be.
It couldn't be.

But it was.

She leaned closer, hands trembling now, and gently pried the brick forward just enough to reach behind it. Her fingers brushed something soft — aged paper wrapped in plastic. She pulled it free, breath caught in her chest.

An envelope.

No name on the front.

She didn't open it right away. She sat with it in her lap for a moment, the way you might sit beside someone who has just told you something sacred. Then, slowly, carefully, she broke the seal.

The handwriting was different — rougher, more angular — but the emotion was there. Immediate. Undeniable.

It was Jamie.
Writing to Ellie.
Hidden behind a brick, just like the letter she found in her apartment.

She read the letter once. Then again. And again, slower. The words clung to her ribs. The love in them — bruised and bewildered and still alive — cracked something open inside her.

Dear Ellie,

You were never too much.
Not too emotional. Not too impulsive. Not too loud or soft or strange.
You were color in a world I didn't realize had gone grey.

I keep thinking I'll walk into a room and you'll be there—elbow on the counter, that half-smile like you know something I don't.
But it's always just me. And the quiet.

I still make enough tea for two. Still look for you in poems I don't understand until I pretend you wrote them.

You were just enough. Always enough.
And I would've loved you every day you let me.

Love,
Jamie

Maisie swallowed hard, blinking against the blur rising behind her eyes. The letter didn't feel like it had been written twenty years ago. It felt like it had been written for her. For right now.

She thought of Carter. His calculated charm. The way he never quite saw her. The cultivated life they had built like a perfectly arranged bookshelf — elegant, symmetrical, hollow.

She thought of Rex, who offered her lavender and quiet and a kind of stillness that made her feel seen without performance.

And she thought of Ellie. Of the mural. Of the words that kept looping in her mind. Words of regret. Words of longing.

Maisie folded the letter carefully and slid it back into the envelope. She held it for a long moment, feeling the weight of it — not ready to let it go, but not sure what to do with it yet.

She wasn't sure what came next.

But for the first time in a long time, she was certain it had to be different.

23 YOU WON'T

He found her sitting in the courtyard again, but this time she wasn't still.
Her hands were tangled in her lap, fingers knotted like they were holding something in. Her knees were drawn up slightly, and her gaze — usually soft, thoughtful — was glassy, far away. Not reading. Not thinking. Just spinning.

Rex paused a few feet away, not wanting to startle her. He'd seen people come undone before — angry, loud, sharp-edged. Maisie was the opposite. She was unraveling inward.

"You alright?" he asked gently.

She looked up slowly, as if surfacing from underwater. Her eyes met his, and she blinked once. Then again. "No," she said. "Not really."

He walked closer, not pushing. Just present.

"Can I sit?" he asked.

She nodded.

He sat beside her on the low stone wall, careful to leave just enough space. The garden smelled like damp soil and lilacs. Somewhere above them, wind moved through the trees.

For a long moment, they just sat.

Then, quietly, Maisie said, "I found a second letter."

Rex turned slightly toward her. "From Ellie?"

"No. From Jamie." She exhaled like the words weighed something. "He hid it too. Behind a brick in the garden. I wasn't looking. I swear I wasn't. But it was there. Like it was waiting."

Rex didn't say anything at first. Then, quietly, he said, "What are the chances?"

Maisie's voice cracked. "He loved her. He never stopped. And she—" She swallowed. "She didn't leave because she stopped loving him. She left because she thought she had to. Because she was afraid. And now it might be too late."

She pressed her palms to her eyes. "I don't know why it matters so much, but it does. I have to find him, Rex. For her. For them. So she knows... it wasn't wasted. That it was real. That it mattered."

He watched her quietly, heart tightening. She looked wrecked and luminous all at once — like someone mid-transformation, not broken but breaking open.

"Then let's find him," he said.

She looked at him, eyes wide and wet. "You'd help me?"

"I'd do more than that," he said, voice low. "But one step at a time."

Maisie gave a soft laugh — more exhale than sound — and shook her head. "I don't get you."

"What's there to get?"

"You're just... steady. I feel like I'm unraveling and you're just sitting there, calm, like I won't fall apart if you're nearby."

He looked at her then, really looked. "You won't."

A long pause hung between them. Then, slowly, she reached out —

not for comfort, not for drama — just to place her hand on his, fingers light but certain.

He didn't move.

Didn't say a word.

He just let her stay there.

And in that moment, it was enough.

24 THE SEARCH

She couldn't sleep that night.

The letter sat on her nightstand, folded carefully, untouched since the courtyard. She kept glancing at it like it might vanish. Like she'd dreamt it.

Jamie had written to Ellie. Jamie had loved her still.

Maisie replayed that moment in the garden over and over — the soft, trembled way Ellie had said *"I lost him. Not just emotionally. I mean... really lost him."* There was no bitterness in her voice. Only the quiet devastation of someone who had made peace with grief by naming it permanent.

But he'd written. He'd waited. Maybe not forever, but long enough to matter.

And now Maisie had to find him. For Ellie. *For herself.*

She started the next morning with coffee and her laptop at the kitchen table, her hair still damp and unbrushed. Carter had left early for a brunch meeting with someone named Blaine or Grant — she hadn't bothered to keep track.

Maisie pulled up a blank document and started typing anything she could remember about Jamie from the letters. There wasn't much.

- Jamie Reed.

- Artist.

- Lived in the building maybe 15-20 years ago?

- Painted the mural on 14th & Mercer.

- Possibly connected to a community co-op or poetry events.

She sipped her coffee, fingers hovering over the keys.

Then she searched: **"Mural 14th & Mercer NYC artist"**

A few clicks in, she found a blog post from nearly a decade ago: *Urban Memory: Preserving Forgotten Street Art*. It featured a photograph of the mural — younger, brighter — and a caption: *"Untitled piece, East Village, believed to be painted by local artist J. Reed around 2007. Artist reportedly moved out of the city shortly after."*

Maisie stared at the name.
J. Reed. Jamie Reed.

There was no link, no contact. Just a whisper of a name.

She searched again — **Jamie Reed artist** — and filtered by location. Dozens of hits. Painters. Musicians. A taxidermist.

Then one caught her eye: *Jamie Reed, upstate NY. Teaches community art classes at the Red Barn Studio. Occasional exhibitions: portraiture and large-scale mixed media.*

She clicked the link.

There was a headshot — grainy, off-center. But something about the eyes felt known to her.

Maisie's breath caught.

It was him.

According to the article, he'd relocated upstate years ago. Taught community art classes. Painted murals on library walls, community centers, even a fire station. The piece described his work as "intimate, reflective, and rich with memory — like someone painting from a place that still hurt, but no longer bled."

Maisie stared at the photo, mesmerized.

He hadn't vanished.

He had simply made a quieter life.

She didn't know what to do with this yet. Didn't know if she should tell Ellie. If she *could*. If it would help, or hurt, or crack something open that had long been sealed shut.

She needed to tell someone. But not Carter. Never Carter.

So she slipped on a sweater, stepped into her shoes, and walked down to the courtyard, hoping to find Rex.

He was there. Kneeling in the dirt, coaxing a row of stubborn tulips into position.

She stood a few feet away, watching him. He hadn't noticed her yet. She realized she could leave, say nothing, keep it all to herself. But then he looked up — and the calm in his face, the steadiness, anchored her.

"Hey," she said, voice low.

"Hey," he answered, brushing soil from his hands.

"I found him," she said.

Rex straightened. "Jamie?"

She nodded.

A beat passed between them.

"He's alive," she said. "He's in the Hudson Valley. Teaching art. It's got to be him."

Rex's expression didn't change. Just a small nod, a quiet breath.

Maisie nodded in return. "I don't know if I should tell her."

He looked at her then — not with advice or answers, but with presence. "You will. When it's time."

Maisie stepped closer, folding her arms. "I don't know why this matters so much to me."

Rex gave a half-smile. "I think you do."

She looked at him.

"You want to believe it's not too late," he said softly. "For them. For you."

Maisie's throat tightened.

"Yeah," she whispered. "I do."

They stood in the garden, the ivy curling around old brick, the mural watching in silence from the alley wall.

She didn't know what came next. But she wasn't afraid of it anymore.

25 FINDING JAMIE

She didn't tell Ellie.

Not yet.

It felt too fragile. Like holding a bird that might die if startled.

Instead, she packed a weekend bag and told Carter she needed space. He barely looked up from his phone.

Maisie took the early train north, the Hudson River unspooling beside her like a ribbon of stillness. She hadn't been out of the city in months. Years, maybe. Trees gave way to fields. Steel gave way to wood.

She clutched the envelope Jamie had written, folded neatly in her coat pocket. Her hands wouldn't stop fidgeting with it.

When she stepped off the train in Hudson, the air felt different. Cleaner. Less urgent. She took a slow breath and followed the walking directions she'd scribbled down.

Red Barn Studio.
That's what the website said.
No phone number. No email. Just come if you want.

Maisie crossed a gravel path and found herself standing before an old red building with a sloping roof and a crooked porch. A sign hung loosely by the door, hand-painted but fading: Art Is What Remains.

Her heart knocked once, twice, then steadied.

She stepped inside.

The room smelled of turpentine, sawdust, and something warm — like woodsmoke or old sun. Paintings lined the walls — abstract forms, portraits, brushstrokes that felt like memory. A few people chatted quietly near easels in the back.

Then she saw him.

At a worktable near the window. Gray at the temples. Stubble on his jaw. A quiet gravity to the way he stood — like someone who had lived with silence long enough to stop resisting it.

Jamie.

Maisie's throat tightened.

She took a slow step forward.

"Jamie Reed?"

He turned, surprised but not startled. "Yes?"

She opened her mouth. Closed it. Then finally:

"My name is Maisie. I... I live in your old building. In the East Village."

His expression didn't change, but something in his eyes shifted. Like the past had just walked through the door.

She took another step. "I found a letter. Hidden behind a brick in the garden wall."

Jamie didn't move.

"It was for Ellie."

At that, he sat down slowly on the edge of the table.

"I didn't think anyone would ever find that," he said.

Maisie held it out.

He looked at her. Really looked.

A long silence bloomed between them. Not empty — full. Of time. Regret. Memory.

"I met her," Maisie said softly. "She's at Bellwood Haven now. She's… older. Quiet. But she remembers you."

Jamie closed his eyes for a moment, then nodded. "She always said love was too big for her. Too messy. She needed her life neat. Predictable."

Maisie's voice caught. "She loved you. She just didn't know how to hold it."

He opened his eyes. They were damp. "That makes two of us."

Maisie sat in the chair across from him. Neither of them spoke for a while.

Then Jamie whispered, "Is she okay?"

Maisie nodded. "She has some health issues, but I think she will be. I think she's waiting for something. Even if she doesn't know it."

Jamie looked out the window, where late light poured through a stand of trees. "Sometimes I still paint her. In pieces. The curve of her jaw. The look she gave me when she thought I was saying something worth remembering."

Maisie smiled. "You painted a whole mural."

He laughed, just barely. "That was me trying not to drown."

They sat there, quiet again, until Jamie asked, "Do you think she'd want to see me?"

Maisie didn't answer right away. Then she said, "I think there's still time."

Jamie looked down at his hands, then back at her.

"Thank you," he said. "For finding me."

Maisie felt the weight in her chest begin to lift. Just a little.

"For what it's worth," she said, standing slowly, "I think love is always messy. But maybe that's the point."

He nodded once, and she saw it — the ghost of hope, rising carefully in his eyes.

26 IT'S BEEN A LONG WINTER

She didn't call ahead.

Ellie was in the garden again, wrapped in a soft shawl the color of antique lace, her hands resting in her lap like they were holding something invisible.

Maisie approached slowly, her heart pattering against her ribs. Her fingers brushed the letter in her coat pocket — Jamie's letter. The one Ellie never read.

"Ellie?"

The older woman turned. Her eyes, still sharp, settled on Maisie with the cautious warmth of someone learning to trust again.

Maisie offered a small smile. "Hi again."

Ellie's expression softened. "You came back."

"I did," Maisie said, her voice gentle. "I wasn't sure I should, but... I have something for you."

She sat beside her and placed the envelope in Ellie's hands without a word.

Ellie stared at it for a moment. Her fingers shook.

She opened it slowly, as if afraid the paper might crumble. She read silently. Once. Twice. A breath held. Then released.

When she finished, her hand came to her mouth. Ellie blinked hard. "How did you—?"

"I found it. Behind a brick in the courtyard. Just like yours."

Ellie's eyes searched hers. "Why does this matter so much to you?"

"Because I know what it's like to be with someone who checks all the boxes, who looks perfect on paper... but never really sees you. And I've been telling myself that's enough. That comfort and status and predictability are love. But then I read your letter. And Jamie's." She paused, voice tightening. "And I realized what you had was real. Messy, imperfect — but real. And it scared me how easily I could miss something like that. How easily I already might have."

Ellie was quiet for a long time.

Then she asked, barely above a whisper, "Is he...?"

Maisie reached into her coat again and pulled out a small photo. She'd printed it the night before — the one from the Red Barn Studio's website.

Ellie took it like it might burn her. Her hand covered her mouth again, but her eyes... they widened, softened, filled with something Maisie hadn't seen before.

"He's alive," Maisie said. "He's still painting. Still remembering you."

Ellie stared at the photo, the way someone might stare at a door that had just creaked open after being shut for twenty years.

Maisie reached out, gently placing her hand over Ellie's. "You don't have to do anything. You don't owe anyone anything. But if there's even the smallest part of you that wants to see him... I can bring him to you."

Ellie didn't speak. But she didn't let go of the photo either.

Her thumb moved gently along the edge, tracing the curve of Jamie's face. Her lips parted, then closed again, as if language had become something fragile — something she had to re-learn.

Maisie waited. She didn't rush her. The silence wasn't empty. It was full. Of years. Of longing. Of the ache of unfinished love.

Then, finally, Ellie spoke.

"I used to dream of this," she whispered, eyes still on the photo. "Not every night. But enough. Just… seeing his face again. Hearing his voice. Knowing he didn't forget."

She swallowed, her voice barely holding.

"I thought I lost the right to ask for that."

Maisie shook her head. "You never did."

Ellie looked up then, and for the first time, Maisie saw something in her that hadn't been there before — a flicker of hope, trembling but alive.

"I want to see him," Ellie said. The words were simple, but they came out like a vow. "Not someday. Not when I've worked up the nerve. I want to see him *now*. Before I forget how to feel something this big."

Maisie smiled, her throat tight.

"Then we'll make it happen."

Ellie folded the photo carefully, placed it back in the envelope alongside the letter, and held them both against her chest like a prayer.

Her voice was steadier now. "Tell him… if he still wants to see me, I'll be here. In a different garden, but with the same stubborn ivy. A little slower, maybe. A little more silver. But I'll be here."

Maisie nodded, blinking fast.

Ellie looked up at the sky, the breeze lifting her braid gently over her shoulder.

"It's been a long winter," she said softly. "I'd like a spring."

And with that, the door that had stayed shut for two decades creaked open — not with force, but with grace.

And Ellie… stepped toward it.

27 TWENTY YEARS, ONE TOMORROW

It had been decided.
Jamie would come to Bellwood Haven the next day.

Maisie and Rex had made the arrangements quietly, without fanfare
— just a phone call, a time, a soft-spoken yes. Jamie's voice on the
line had trembled, steady but unsure, like a man bracing himself for
something sacred.

He didn't ask what to say.
He only asked, *"Will she want to see me?"*

Maisie had answered without hesitation.
"She already does."

That morning, Maisie arrived at Bellwood Haven with a small bag of
things Ellie had requested — hand cream, a light rose lipstick, and
the same lavender tea she used to drink every afternoon in that ivy-
covered courtyard all those years ago. She found Ellie in her room,
sitting in a cushioned armchair by the window, staring out as if
trying to memorize the shape of the sky.

Ellie didn't turn when she spoke. "I didn't sleep."

Maisie set the bag down gently on the dresser. "Understandable."

Ellie nodded, her fingers twitching slightly in her lap. "It's been twenty years. What does someone say after that much silence?"

Maisie walked to the window, kneeling so they were eye to eye. "You say what's true. That's always enough."

Ellie blinked hard, her eyes glassy. "What if the words don't come?"

Maisie smiled softly. "Then you let him speak first."

Later that afternoon, Ellie grew quiet and unusually fussy. She turned away the soup brought to her room, complained of a headache, and said the lighting was "too harsh, too yellow — makes me look like a ghost."

When Maisie offered to turn on the bedside lamp instead, Ellie waved her off. "I should've had my hair done. I look like a widow who lost the war."

Maisie chuckled. "You look beautiful. And human. Which is better."

Ellie reached for the lipstick in the bag and turned it in her hand like a relic. "I don't know what I thought this would feel like. Closure, maybe. Peace. But instead, I feel... like a girl again. Nauseous and full of too many feelings."

"You're allowed to feel all of it," Maisie said gently.

Ellie pressed her lips together. "I never thought I'd see him again. Never let myself imagine it. And now I can't stop imagining everything. How he'll look. How he'll smell. What he'll see when he looks at me."

Maisie hesitated, then knelt again beside the chair. "He's not coming to see a version of you. He's coming to see *you*. All of you. Still."

That softened something. Not entirely. But enough.

In the early evening, Ellie asked to go outside, bundled in her shawl and slowly navigating the garden path with her walker. Maisie sat nearby as Ellie adjusted her seat and tilted her face toward the sky.

The sun hung low, spilling a gentle gold over the flowerbeds and fountains.

"I don't know what I'll say," Ellie murmured. "Maybe I won't say anything. Maybe I'll just look at him and let it be."

Maisie reached out and tucked a loose strand of silver hair behind her ear. "That would be enough."

Ellie closed her eyes and let the breeze brush against her cheek.

"I used to think I needed to be perfect to be loved like that. Now I just hope he still sees me in all this... fadedness."

Maisie's voice was soft. "He will."

That night, Maisie texted Rex:
She's ready. Nervous, but ready.

He wrote back: **He's packed. Shirt with no wrinkles. Poem in his wallet. I'll drive him up at 10.**

Maisie smiled, her heart full and tender.

Tomorrow, two people who had once lost everything would find out what remained.

And maybe, just maybe...
it would be everything.

28 LOVE, ELLIE

The ride was quiet, but not tense.

Jamie sat in the back seat, hands clasped loosely in his lap, a bouquet of wildflowers resting beside him. He'd picked them himself — said he didn't want store-bought. Said he remembered how Ellie once said that real beauty grows from chaos.

Maisie drove, with Rex in the passenger seat beside her. The spring morning was soft and bright, the kind that made everything seem possible.

Jamie wore a pressed blue shirt, slightly wrinkled at the elbows. His beard had been neatly trimmed. He had barely spoken, but the emotion behind his silence filled the car.

When they passed the first sign for Bellwood Haven, he finally spoke.

"I dreamed about this last night," he said quietly. "About seeing her again. Her hair was silver, but her eyes were the same. She laughed when she saw me."

Maisie glanced at him in the rearview mirror, smiling gently. "She's been waiting, Jamie."

He nodded, a trembling breath in his chest. "So have I."

They pulled into the gravel lot just after ten. The garden was already beginning to hum with bees and birdsong, the ivy on the front wall curling upward like memory.

Jamie stepped out slowly, clutching the bouquet in one hand, his other pressed briefly to his chest, as if steadying something inside him.

But before they reached the front door, a nurse stepped out onto the porch. She looked pale, like someone had just extinguished a light she hadn't realized was so close to burning out.

"Are you here to see Eleanor Hart?" she asked gently.

Maisie nodded. "Yes. We called ahead—"

The nurse's voice was careful, but her words cracked the air.

"I'm… I'm so sorry. Ms. Hart passed away in her sleep last night. Peacefully. Very peacefully."

Jamie stopped walking.

Maisie felt her heart drop like a stone.

"What?" she whispered. "No… she was fine yesterday. She was nervous. She—she was ready."

The nurse nodded slowly, her eyes shining. "She was ready. She told me so. She asked for her favorite tea. She said it felt like spring."

Jamie stood frozen, the flowers dangling from his hand. He didn't speak.

Maisie turned to him, her voice breaking. "Oh, Jamie… I'm so sorry."

The nurse looked up suddenly, eyes narrowing. "Jamie?" she asked.

Maisie nodded. "Yes… this is him."

The nurse blinked back emotion. "There was a letter. On her nightstand. She'd been writing it last night. It's addressed to Jamie. Would you… would you like it?"

Jamie nodded, but he couldn't speak.

She returned a moment later with a folded piece of stationery. His name was written on the front in careful, wavering script.

He took it in both hands like it might vanish.

Dear Jamie,

I don't know if you'll ever read this.

Maybe I'm writing it just to get the thoughts out of my head and onto paper — a way to steady myself before tomorrow.

I'm restless tonight. I'm too full of the kind of hope I thought I'd left behind years ago. The kind that keeps you up counting possibilities instead of sheep.

I'm going to see you tomorrow.

Can you believe that?

After everything — the years, the silence, the weight of what we never said — we are finally going to be in the same place again. Not as ghosts. Not as memories. But as people with beating hearts and soft hands and things still left to say.

I don't know what I'll say, Jamie.

Maybe I'll apologize again. Maybe I'll cry. Maybe I'll reach for your hand like no time had passed at all.

Mostly, I think I'll just look at you.
Let myself *really* look.

And I hope that you'll look at me, too, and still see the girl who stood in your kitchen barefoot, quoting Neruda and pretending not to love you yet.

I have regretted leaving you every day. Not because I didn't build a life — I did. But because that life never hummed the way it did when you were near. You were music. You were ache. You were color in the corners of a world I tried too hard to tidy up.

I don't know if I'll be brave enough to say all this out loud tomorrow. But just in case I'm not — I want to say it here:

I never stopped loving you.
Not once.
Not even when I was afraid to say it out loud.

Maybe this is just for me. Maybe this is the only way I know how to show up right now.

No more silence. No more brick walls.

Only this:

You were the best part.
You always were.

Love,
Ellie

Jamie stood on the porch a long time after he finished reading. The sun had risen fully by then, and the garden below swayed with the breath of spring.

He didn't cry.

He just closed his eyes, held the letter to his chest, and whispered to the breeze, "I see you, Ellie."

And somewhere, in that quiet bloom of morning, the ivy kept growing anyway.

29 THE DECISION

The apartment felt different when Maisie walked back through the door. It wasn't just that it was quiet — it had always been quiet — but that now the silence didn't soothe her. It pressed against her like an accusation.

She left her bag by the door and drifted into the living room. The stillness felt artificial, like a room waiting to be photographed. Everything was where it should be — the cushions fluffed just right, the books on the coffee table fanned out in neat symmetry. She'd once thought it elegant. Now it just felt contrived. Staged.

A life arranged like furniture.

Carter came home an hour later. His tie was loose, and his smile was automatic.

"There you are," he said. "You didn't text back."

Maisie looked at him, her expression unreadable. "I needed time."

He stepped closer, looking genuinely concerned. "Is everything okay?"

Maisie hesitated. "I went to see someone. Her name is Ellie."

Carter blinked. "Who?"

"She's the woman who wrote the letter. I found her."

He looked confused, as if she were telling him a story in a language he didn't speak. "Maisie, why does this matter so much to you?"

Maisie walked to the window, arms crossed. "Because her story is mine. Or at least, it could be. She was me — someone who stayed quiet, who picked the safe life, who walked away from something real."

Carter's voice sharpened slightly. "You think this life we've built isn't real?"

She turned to face him. "It's beautiful. It's functional. But it's not love."

Silence fell between them.

He sat down, as if the weight of her words pushed him back. "I love you, Maisie. I've built everything around you. Around us."

"I know," she said, her voice soft. "But you love the version of me that fits into your world. The version that looks good beside you at charity galas and on social media. I don't know if you've ever really seen me."

He stared at her. "And who's seeing you now?"

Maisie didn't answer immediately. She didn't need to. The silence was answer enough.

Carter exhaled, standing again. "Is there someone else?"

Maisie shook her head. "There's someone who listened. Someone who didn't need me to be anything but who I am."

"You're throwing everything away over a letter?"

"I'm choosing not to make the same mistake Ellie made," she said.

"She let fear win. I won't."

Carter's voice broke, just slightly. "We were happy."

Maisie's eyes welled. "We were comfortable. That's not the same thing."

He walked past her, standing at the edge of the room, one hand braced against the bookshelf. "So what happens now?"

Maisie reached for the ring on her finger. Her hands shook as she slipped it off. She walked to the kitchen island and placed it gently on the marble surface.

"I'm going to pack a few things," she said. "And then I'm going to figure out what comes next."

That night, she stayed in a hotel across town. Nothing fancy. A room with a window overlooking a noisy street and the faint sound of traffic rising like white noise. She sat on the bed with Ellie's poem beside her and began to write in her own notebook for the first time in months.

She wrote about silence, about doubt, about all the times she'd bent herself into shapes that pleased other people. And then she wrote about Ellie. And Jamie. And Rex.

And herself.

The next morning, she returned to the apartment to grab the rest of her things. Carter wasn't there. Just the faint scent of lemon cleaner and the sound of the clock ticking.

Maisie moved quietly through the space, packing a few books, some clothes, her journals. She paused at the bookshelf, running her hand along the spines of the novels she once displayed for guests — the ones she hadn't read, but knew made her look well-read.

She left them.

By the time she shut the door behind her, she felt lighter. Not free, exactly. But close.

She pulled out her phone and sent a single text to Rex:

Do you have time for coffee?

The reply came almost instantly:

Always.

Maisie smiled.

It wasn't a perfect ending. It wasn't even an ending.

But it was a beginning.

30   THE LEAP

The café was small, tucked between a used vinyl shop and a bodega with faded fruit crates out front. Maisie pushed open the door and was met with the scent of fresh espresso and something sugary baking in the back. Jazz played low over the speakers — soft horns and slow piano — and it felt like the kind of place where you could breathe without apology.

Rex was already there. He sat by the window, his denim jacket folded neatly over the back of the chair, a coffee mug in his hand. When he looked up and saw her, he didn't smile broadly or stand with a dramatic gesture. He simply offered the warmest, calmest look she'd seen in weeks — like he'd been waiting for her, but wasn't surprised she came.

"Hi," she said.

"Hey."

She slid into the seat across from him. For a few seconds, they just sat there, letting the quiet settle around them.

"I left him," Maisie said finally. "It's done."

Rex gave a small nod. "How do you feel?"

Maisie exhaled slowly. "Like I finally stopped pretending."

He didn't rush to respond, didn't fill the space with platitudes or reassurances. Instead, he reached across the table and set his hand gently over hers. His palm was rough, warm. Grounding.

"I'm proud of you," he said.

Maisie looked out the window. The city still buzzed around them — traffic honking, people rushing, life moving forward — but she felt strangely still. Like she'd stepped off a treadmill and found solid ground for the first time in a long while.

"I don't know what happens next," she admitted. "I don't have a plan."

Rex chuckled. "Plans are overrated. But if it helps — you're not alone."

She blinked hard, the weight of that simple sentence hitting her deeper than she expected.

They sipped their coffee and talked. About everything and nothing. About Ellie and Jamie. About books they loved. About gardens and childhood and the things they used to dream about before life told them to pick something practical.

Maisie told him about the poem Ellie gave her. She pulled the folded page from her purse and laid it on the table.

If I could do it over,
I'd stay in the room.
I'd speak the words.
I'd let the silence break me open.

Rex read it twice. "That's the real kind of bravery, isn't it? Staying. Speaking."

Maisie nodded. "She ran. She couldn't speak her truth. I almost didn't speak mine. But I found her just in time."

"You found yourself."

She met his eyes, and for the first time in weeks, she didn't look away.

The days that followed didn't fall into perfect order. Maisie didn't wake up with everything fixed or certain. But things felt... honest. She found a temporary apartment on the west side — small, sunny, full of strange angles and secondhand charm. She bought mismatched mugs, cooked grilled cheese for dinner, and played her old records too loud.

Rex came over most nights. Sometimes they talked for hours. Sometimes they didn't talk at all. And it was enough.

Maisie wrote every morning — not about weddings or expectations, but about freedom, about bravery, about love. Her notebook filled with raw, tangled paragraphs and half-finished poems. She didn't write them for anyone else.

Just for her.

EPILOGUE

Six months later

The apartment was smaller. The ceilings were lower. The windows didn't frame skyline views or glimmering city lights. But there were plants on every sill, books stacked in uneven towers, and music playing from a crackly old record player that only worked when you nudged it just right.

Maisie loved every imperfect inch of it.

Rex sat at the kitchen table, scribbling notes for a community garden project he was trying to start on an abandoned lot down the street. He wore the same faded denim jacket he always had, and when he looked up and smiled at her, it still caught her off guard — not because it was dazzling, but because it was real.

Maisie was at her desk, hunched over a notebook, ink staining her fingers.

She was writing again.

Letters, mostly. Some to people she knew. Some to people she never intended to send. Some to her younger self. And some — still — to Ellie.

Joy at Bellwood Haven had come across a postcard addressed to Maisie and forwarded it along — a serene image of the koi pond, with a few deliberate words written in elegant script.:

The lavender you brought is blooming. I hope you are too.
— Ellie

Maisie pressed the card to her chest and closed her eyes.

She thought of Jamie sometimes — the man Ellie had loved. She wondered how he was doing.

But Maisie never reached out. She didn't need to. Some stories weren't meant to be picked back up — only passed forward.

Apartment 4B had new tenants now. A young couple in their twenties — idealistic, impatient, tender in the way only first-time cohabiters can be. They had painted the living room a bold green and strung Edison bulbs across the balcony.

One afternoon, while setting up a shelf, they knocked a loose brick near the radiator.

The woman reached in.

Her fingers closed around something unexpected — soft, folded, left behind.

She pulled out the letter carefully, tied with a faded green ribbon.

There was no return address. No explanation.

Only a name. And a story waiting to be remembered.

LOVE, ELLIE

ABOUT THE AUTHOR

H. Moore is a Canadian writer and the author of several nonfiction titles. Love, Ellie is her first work of fiction—and her first foray into romance.

Manufactured by Amazon.ca
Bolton, ON

46331074R00072